Nicholas House is a British born writ
South of England. He took up writin
by the stories of Jules Verne and H.G

CW00385285

Fascinated by the natural world he went on to study Geosciences at university. This afforded him the chance to travel and fuel his over active imagination, allowing him to take inspiration from a vast array of varied sources.

He went on to merge his passion for writing and love for video production by creating scripted videos on YouTube which continues to let him experiment with a variety of writing styles.

Primarily writing Supernatural Fantasy and Science Fiction, Nicholas has also written numerous pieces of published poetry alongside short stories, e-books and scientific articles. With a mind so full of ideas and an ongoing literary passion he plans to continue writing about whatever inspires him long into the future.

Also by Nicholas House

Novels
Chronicles of the Median

Novellas
The Dark
Illumination

Collections
Abridged: A Short Collection of Short Stories

Abridged
A Short Collection of Short Stories

Nicholas House

Abridged: A Short Collection of Short Stories
Copyright© 2013, 2020 Nicholas House

Contents

Around the Galaxy in 80 Days

Somewhere on the outskirts of London, England, at some point in the future, no one was entirely sure exactly when, it rained. It rained especially heavy that night on Chapel Street, partly to create an air of inauspicious mystery but mainly because the local council hadn't gotten around to repairing the weather regulator yet. In that street the only house that seemed to have semblance of life about it was number 37. There was a kind of dull, warm glow about the building and it seemed to have somewhat of an inviting quality to it. Inside sat four old men, each sipping gently on brandy from large Snifters. Then there was another, much younger, man slurping loudly on a lager from a dented can with one hand whilst trying to handle a poorly constructed Lamp Kebab with the other. This mans name was Gerald Tansem, yet for reasons that never truly became clear to anyone, he preferred to be called Shwaps. Contrary to the belief of most, if not all, of his peers he had recently become the newest member of The Educated Guild of Travellers. Despite the fact that efficient interstellar space travel had been achieved decades ago and was now readily available to the masses, no one really travelled anymore. In light of this the entry requirements for the guild had been somewhat reduced and seeing as Shwaps was the only one who bothered to turn up for a school trip to Saturn's rings when he was eleven, he more then qualified for acceptance.

"Yes, Sidney," chuckled one of the older men, swirling his brandy slowly, "you may have travelled to the systems deepest pit on Ganymede, but I have travelled as far as the Great Seas of Blessed."

"Indeed," began another old man, already with a deep air of condescension, "I, however, have travelled to the galactic rim and I tell you, the food out there can make you sick for a month."

Shwaps suddenly took notice of what was being said and put his kebab on a greasy piece of paper in his lap. "You mean they've got McDerik's on the edge of the galaxy?" his voice was steady and serious, echoing around the room as the light chuckling fell silent.

Another of the old men, this one possessing an overly large beard, took a long sip of his brandy only to seem astonished when his glass was emptied. "So, Gerald," he muttered after an uncomfortably long pause, "where exactly have you been, of late?" he got up out of his deep red leather backed chair and poured himself another glass out of a crystal flask.

"Um," he took another bite from his kebab before holding it up, speaking with a full mouth, "went to the kebab shop before coming here."

"I think he means have you been anywhere you have to genuinely travel to?" added the only one who had not contributed to the conversation yet.

"Um..." Shwaps thought hard, with the strain of the exercise clearly showing.

"Nowhere, that's where!" snapped the man who had visited the Great Seas of Blessed. "I don't know why you were allowed to join in the first place!"

"I've been to Saturn!" Shwaps tried, "and I bet I could go as far as Mr. 'The food is disgusting nine and a half thousand light years away'," he replied clumsily yet managing to leave at least two of the men shocked and insulted.

"Fine! Let us place a wager. A wager that you can not travel..." the old man thought for a second of a suitable and equally impossible endeavour, "around the galaxy in, oh let's keep with tradition, eighty days."

"Eighty days?" Shwaps repeated uneasily, "You do realise how big the galaxy actually is, don't you?"

The men around him grinned. "Well, if you don' think you can manage it then you are clearly not the traveller you claim to be and you know where the door is," they all looked in sequence to the front door expectantly.

Shwaps considered their proposition for a second but before he could come to a decision his mouth opened. "You're on!" something inside him was surprised that he had agreed to something virtually impossible, especially after that time with the Llamas. "What're we betting?"

"Well, let's see. If you can not achieve this feat then you will have to leave this club and reimburse us for all of the things that you have ingested, broken and...err," The old man coughed nervously, "disgraced."

"And if I win," he clapped his hands together and got up, putting his kebab on the seat along with the can of larger on the arm of the chair, "I get to stay in this cushy little number with a reward of five grand. Five thousand quid! Five- zero- zero- zero smackaroons," naturally he made a large emphasis on the amount of money he wanted.

The men murmured among themselves for a few seconds before looking up calmly. "Fine, we have a wager, then?"

"Yeah, we got a *wager*," Shwaps slapped his hand against the old mans and shook hard leaving an unsettling grease stain in his palm. He then rushed towards the dark teak door leading out on to the wet street. Grabbing the knob, he swung the door open fiercely and stormed out. Seconds later the door swung back open to reveal Shwaps again, drenched from the rain. He gave the group of old men a quick, weary glance, leaned round the back of the door and snatched away his leather jacket.

"Be back here at exactly," the old man who had suggested the bet looked at a posh digital clock in a mahogany case which read ten to midnight, "exactly twelve midnight."

"Right," Shwaps put his jacket on in an over exaggerated way and once again exited the building, this time not to return.

"Well," said one of the old men who had now emptied just over five glasses of brandy, "that's the last we'll see of him."

"I would say he won't even get to the space port. We shall never have to see him again," he grinned subtly. "No more broken ornaments, no more food stains," he was stopped by an odd smell emanating from where Shwaps had been sitting. Looking down he saw the remnants of the kebab mixed with the larger that, he now realized, Shwaps had knocked over whilst putting his jacket on. He sighed in dismay at the infernal concoction slowly soaking through its multi-layered packaging and irreversibly staining the plush chair. "I pray to god he doesn't make it."

Shwaps hammered on a flimsy red door along a narrow, somewhat less privileged, street. Here, at least, the weather regulator was working and so it wasn't raining. After a few minutes of uninterrupted banging a light appeared through the arched window at the top of the door. Numerous bolts were soon thrown back and chains rattled as they were hurriedly undone before the door was opened with lightning speed.

"What do ya' want!?" there was a silhouette of an average built individual grasping a baseball bat tightly, poised to swing as hard as it dared.

"Phil! Watch what you're doin' with that thing!" Shwaps grabbed the bat and wrestled it off Phil without much resistance.

"Shwaps? What the hell are you doing here?" he looked at the pitch-black sky then down the lightless street, "and at this time of night?"

"I need you to get me tickets to the Triton Space Port," babbled Shwaps.

"What? Slow down," Phil rubbed his eyes in bewilderment, "Triton? That port's for interstellar travel. Why do you want to go interstellar?"

"A bet," Shwaps barged his way past Phil only to begin rummaging through the nearest draw, "a bet that I can't get around the galaxy in eighty days."

"How drunk are you?" queried Phil loudly in an attempt to distract his friend from searching through his possessions.

"I'm not," Shwaps replied, withdrawing quickly with Phil's passport in hand.

"Why have you got-... No, I'm not coming with you, you can forget it!"

"Yes, you are, every traveller needs a passport," mistook Shwaps.

"However much you *do* need a passport, I think you mean a Passepartout. I'm still not coming with-"

"I'll share my ten grand reward with you," Shwaps lied, knowing very well that the only thing that could sway Phil's decision was the idea of money going his way.

There was a second of stunned silence as Phil flicked his eyes around curiously. "I'm coming with you," he was about to step out from the door when a cold gust of wind blew, its chill reminding Phil that he was still only wearing a pair of boxer shorts and a baggy shirt. "I'll put some clothes on first, though."

The next morning Shwaps and Phil arrived at the Cape Canaveral Transit Station carrying nothing but the clothes on their backs and a bag of overpriced memorabilia. The Transit Station was large and marginally dome shaped with tall spires reaching to the sky. Occasionally a small craft would emerge from the tip of a seemingly random spire at high speed and race off through the atmosphere.

The lobby had plush marble floors, various flashing signs for people to blatantly ignore and duty free shops packed with people purchasing English alcohol, Spanish alcohol, American alcohol and any other type of alcohol they could get their hands on.

Shwaps, after quite a bit of arguing with the attendant, finally managed to get himself through check-in as anything other then livestock. On the other hand Phil had continually set off the metal detector and was being threatened with a body cavity search until he spontaneously produced a five pence piece which had become stuck in the lining of his coat. Even so, in light of the commotion they had caused, security reasoned they could justify cavity searches for the both of them regardless.

After finally managing to make it through customs they sat in the large, crowded waiting area, staring at the brightly lit billboards for their flight to appear. They did this for a significant amount of time until finally, some three and a half hours later, their flight was illuminated in large green letters. Led by Shwaps, the two of them headed in the direction of the designated gate one hundred and twenty seven. The gates architecture seemed to be loosely based on that of a subway station barring the re-enforced Perspex windows in the ceiling above. The long, train like short-range transit pod sat on some kind of highly magnetic track that its self was sunken into the ground. The high edges were marked distinctly with a fluorescent yellow line as if to encourage drunken idiots to submit themselves for the Darwin Award like any good station does. In the bright sunshine that was pouring through the window above, it was possible to see all the way to the end of the track where it simply appeared to stop. This begged the question of distance verses velocity and other intelligible musings but also the much more important consideration of engine verses not being broken.

Soon the doors to the pod opened and around twenty people, including Shwaps and Phil, began to shove on board as to not miss the chance of getting one of the thirty odd seats. The inside was metallic and Spartan with windows running along each side of the cabin, each of which carried a harsh warning about how not to break the glass in the event of an accident. After all, no one really likes explosive decompression, except those few who are best just to remain anonymous. Just as everyone found an adequate seat the doors slid closed and sealed with a harsh hiss. A loud clank sounded from behind the pod and the ignition tube, laid out far ahead, began to gently rise to some unsettlingly high angle and gave another clank as it stopped. The whole chassis rattled and there was an explosion followed by a deafening roar. The rattling continued as the pod started to move along its track. It moved faster and faster towards the ever nearing sky and that consideration about engines occurred to everyone once more. It was already too late, though, the pod shot out of the launch tube at significantly more then the required escape velocity of eight kilometres per second and ploughed through the atmosphere like a bullet through water.

Once the pod was flying in open space and the whole idea of instantaneous death began to pass it became apparent just how much traffic there was going through the solar system. Most of the traffic was made up of delegates from the Utopia Planitia Commercial Hub and the Ceres based mining city of New Melbourne. The general traffic routes, though, were much less congested and so the journey to Triton Space Port lasted only for around twenty minutes. Still this was as far as Shwaps, or anyone else on the pod for that matter, had ever travelled. This was especially true for Phil who had experienced that feeling as he stepped foot on the Hyper Sonic Jet to America at Heathrow.

Triton was an odd world, greyish like the other cold bodies in the system but with shining caps, tinted pink against Neptune's glow. Across its surface sprawled large networks of domed buildings and cruiser bays with acceleration tubes stretching off in every direction. As soon as they touched down on one of the numerous landing pads, the transfer between the transport pod and the Continental Class Space Liner was, with understatement, more then quick. Put simply the process went thusly; step from pod on to fast moving conveyer belt. Travel through large detector to have vaporised anything that didn't comply with solar law. Finally the belt would lead to a large domed hanger where the huge Space Liner was stood. Everyone would then be hurriedly ushered onto the Liner so that it could launch only two hours behind schedule. After some clearly German fostered efficiency, the last of the passengers boarded and the air locks sealed with triple the amount of clanging and hissing as the pod. The domed roof of the hanger then peeled back and the Liner lifted off, the moons very surface shuddering as the vast ship engaged its Fusion-Ion engines and headed off towards the edge of the Solar System.

After a few seconds of watching the spaceport fall away behind them, the on-board speaker crackled and clicked on. "Welcome, ladies and gentlemen, to the Star Liner Orion. Today's coarse is plotted to the well known star city of Galileo A5, in orbit around the binary stars of the Caster system which lay approximately fifty two light years from Sol. For your comfort, we will be stopping off at Pollex Bed, Breakfast and Service Station at thirty four light years along the route. Until then, please sit back and enjoy your trip." The captains speaker clicked off and the flight attendants emerged, beginning their normal duties of explaining safety. However, the whole part about hallucinogenic fits, in flight meals and brain sucking aliens seemed new. It had clearly been added on account of being the one item left off the safety list to actually occur. To this passengers responded with complete obliviousness or by promptly using all of the in flight sick bags in quick succession because of the overly graphic images now appearing on the plasma screen.

The journey to Pollex was more or less uneventful apart from the school of space dolphins that flew along side the Liner for a few light years. Beyond that Schwaps passed the time sleeping and Phil happily watched the, less than quality, in flight entertainment. Soon enough the Space Liner docked with the service station and everyone was able to leave to use the facilities while the ship re-fuelled.

The space station was like any other bland services and Shwaps, like any other services attendee, spent a few minutes roaming the lobby until he found what he thought was an arcade game. He approached it and pressed the ON button. Nothing happened, so he kicked it. Still nothing happened, so he kicked it again. Yet again, nothing happened. After a while of constant pounding he stopped and gently leaned around the back to see it wasn't even plugged in. "Phil, help me plug this thing in, will you?" Phil complied with Shwaps' request and the screen burst into colour, then faded away with no sound to be heard. The screen remained completely black, then a large amount of yellowish dots, various in size faded into view. Shwaps moved the joystick and jabbed at the buttons which seemed to change the selection of dot, with the joystick moving it around. "What's wrong with this thing?" he said irritably, moving the joystick around and hammering on the buttons, "This game's stupid..."

At the Hubble Association Space Institute a lone researcher sat half asleep in front of a black screen showing only yellowish dots of varying sizes. Each of these dots represented the stars in the night sky, standing as glorious, immovable giants of the cosmos. That was until they began wildly jumping around the screen in all different directions. The researcher slowly opened his eyes and gazed at the screen, bewildered. "There aren't supposed to be any star movements today." The stars continued darting around the screen until they aligned and decided to conduct a rendition of River Dance for a few seconds before returning to their original positions as if nothing had ever occurred.

The researcher squinted and shook his head. "I need another coffee..."

Shwaps had stopped 'Playing' the so called game and had returned to the Liner followed a few minutes later by Phil, his pockets stuffed with junk food he'd spent the whole half hour allocated buying.

The launch from Pollex was much like any other launch, the Liner was delayed several times, a Pollex Weevil was found in the toilet but clearance was eventually received and the ship sped off towards Castor.

Two and a half hours later, some four times longer than most other forms of transport, they reached Castor Star City Galileo A5. As the ship manoeuvred its self for docking, Shwaps marked the distance they had travelled already on a simple map of the galaxy he had torn from one of the in flight magazines. *Fifty two out of seventy thousand light years,* he thought mournfully, *there's not going to be any sight seeing. First things first; rent a car. A Ferrari Comet should do. It's expensive, yeah, and Phil won't like it but, what the hell, he can be ignored.*

Phil was, indeed, ignored and they spent the next four hours travelling along the S.23, S.46, S.52 Spaceways and the fifth Neutron Star Pulse Accelerator until they arrived at New Bigfork, an asteroid settlement off the eastern Cygnus arm intersection. It was much larger then the original Bigfork, despite being comparatively small in its own right. There were around twenty houses, two shops and a small landing pad all surrounding a single public house; The Twilight Inn. Although, so far, they had barely even travelled for one day, they decided a day off was required, even though Shwaps and Phil took 'day off' to loosely mean the better part of a week.

On the last night of their 'well earned' vacation they endeavoured to rid the inn of their alcohol supply as it was supposedly causing issues between tourists and the locals. This was not strictly true but at the very least it was soon to become the general consensus. Among this supply was some of the strongest alcohol in the known galaxy; 'Uncle McPhersons Head Hammering Home Brew'. Subsequently the pair left, or were rather forced to leave, the colony drunker then an Englishman on Saint Patricks day.

Under the influence of alcohol it wasn't the best idea to drive a turbo charged space super car, let alone at speed. Then again, to be fair, they didn't exactly 'speed' per say. They hardly even drove, for that matter. They simply trundled along an empty back space lane, barely over the speed of light, singing songs and telling rude limericks. According to Phil, one such limerick when thusly; "I once knew a robot, his name was Bitties. Then one day his head spun round, his top fell down, and he found out he had-" thankfully the unorthodox non-rhyme was cut short by blue flashing lights in the rear view mirror and a distinct, whirring siren.

The ever so slightly more sober Shwaps pulled the craft over to an oxygenated pod, doing his best to exit the craft and meet the officer without falling down or throwing up.

"Do you realise you were going a bit slow, back there?"

"Was me?" asked Shwaps as soberly as he could.

Phil hiccupped and the officer looked at him quickly. "Are you drunk, sir?"

"No," said Phil, elongating the N, whilst grinning like an idiot. "I'm perfectly drunk," he stopped grinning, "sobrer," he thought very slowly before coming to the conclusion that there was something much more pressing to be addressed. "I jus' wanna stay one thing," his face turned a green colour and his cheeks puffed out, "I'm going to throw up in your hat," he swiped the sturdy fabric hat from the officers head and held it tightly to his face while producing a sickening gurgling noise. Slowly he withdrew it and smiled unsteadily before handing the soggy hat back to the officer. "What do ya know, they're not waterproof," Phil abruptly blacked out, falling rigidly to the ground leaving Shwaps to think it was as good an idea as any before doing so himself.

The next day Shwaps woke up with what felt like an axe protruding from his skull and a vague memory of being sentenced to one month on a prison ship. The charges went something along the lines of drink driving, driving too slow and being sick in an officer of the laws hat. Shwaps sighed. Seven days and he'd already cocked it up more times then France changed sides during wartime. He slumped back onto his bunk and sighed again. He had never actually served jail time before, despite what everyone thought.

All in all, imprisonment hadn't been all too bad for the pair. After all they were on the minimum security deck, surrounded by chocolate bar thieves, other drunks and elderly people who had not paid their television license. Some things they even enjoyed like Tuesday night movies and kebabs at dinner. However, the entire fact that they were in minimum security made it wholly unsurprising when, twelve days later, there happened to be a jail break. It's not even as though Shwaps and Phil wanted any part of it. They just happened to get involved when a screening of 'The Great Escape' got the audience a little over excited. They, along with numerous pseudo-criminals were forced along with the break and ended up having to leave in an escape pod which had a top speed less then a general farm tractor.

At first things were bad, very bad considering the prison ship didn't want to waste the fuel turning around to pick up some trouble makers who simply annoyed the wrong policeman. Things started to look up, though, when the navigation system finally managed to locate its self, managing to lock onto their exact position in the galaxy. Much to Shwaps' delight and Phil's general nonchalance, it had transpired that the prison ship had taken them over thirty thousand light years in the right direction. Right now they were drifting somewhere in the vicinity of the Pegasus Cluster, approximately half way around the galactic bulge and well on their way to victory. However, despite the apparent, unplanned, progress in the past eighteen days, to complete their journey they needed to acquire a craft to travel nearly thirty seven thousand light years in sixty two days. Going on their luck so far this may not have been overly concerning. Only, when considering the fact that they barely had a weeks supply of food and they were no more then a stones throw from the middle of nowhere in what could only be described as a petrol powered box, the situation could have been better.

For a fortnight the pair lived off rationed supplies and packets of peanuts Phil had stolen from the prison cafeteria, drifting in the cramped pod without any semblance of life in the void. Every day they took turns watching the scanner and dodging space junk, until one day, just after the air conditioning had packed in, the scanner picked up something major.

"Shwaps! Wake up!" Phil kicked him in the leg, "wake up!"

"What!?" yelled Shwaps, startled, "what is it?"

"Well, the scanner's picking up something weird. It seems to be some kind of hole. A big grey hole in space," he looked at Shwaps who looked him straight back. He glanced back at the screen with curiosity in his eyes, then wiped it solemnly. "It was steamed up", he mumbled quietly, preparing to be smacked across the back of the head. Suddenly he looked up again, his eyebrows at awkward angles. "Where'd it go?"

Shwaps looked closely at the screen and after a second or two sat back, grimacing at Phil. "What colour is space?"

"Black?" replied Phil cautiously, a touch of a quiver in his voice.

"And what colour, generally, is a Black Hole?"

"Is this a trick question?" he was hit with a forceful stare. "Black?" he endeavoured finally.

"So is it, at all, possible that the anomaly is still out there, that it is a black hole, but you just couldn't see it anymore?" he flicked his eyes towards another panel and sighed, "and now because of this pods somewhat limited detection capabilities we are now too close to the blasted thing to get away."

"Oh," Phil responded simply, not entirely sure how to take the revelation at hand, "what are we going to do?"

"Apart from dying?" Shwaps started unhelpfully, "I imagine we have two options; one: we turn the pod around, shove the engines to full power and try to get out of the gravity well. Granted, before we get barely five thousand metres the engines would of probably burnt out," he said as optimistically as the situation would allow, "or two: we go straight in. According to the readout this thing is big, possibly big enough to be connected to something on the other side. If we're very lucky then we might be dumped in at least a sort of reasonable area."

"How reasonable?" Phil's gaze bore down on Shwaps.

"Best chance is somewhere in this galaxy," his breath hissed through partially gritted teeth, "moderate chance we land in a reality of some shape or form."

"I really can't wait to hear what the worse case is..."

"Well, the worst case is that there's not even an exit to this thing."

"Then what happens?" the pod shook from the gravitational sheer of the black hole, making his words barely understandable.

"Then we get crushed into something the size of an amoeba," Shwaps stuttered less then gently.

"Fine!" Phil conceded, with virtually no thought at all, "I never really liked life anyway," he punched the throttle and the pod jerked around to face the distorted starscape and sped off into the abyss.

As it transpired there *was* something on the other end of the black hole. Against all odds they had even landed in the right reality, somewhere in the Milky Way and even more amazingly both the escape pod and the humans inside had apparently survived.

Nevertheless, the pod was now a wreck. What propulsion there had ever been was effectively gone, most of the oxygen canisters were ruptured and the primary structure of the pod was rapidly disintegrating. With luck now well out of the question and some higher intervention clearly at play, there coincidently happened to be a lone structure barely ten thousand kilometres away from them. The small structure was run down and practically falling apart but still had a neon sign around its landing pad stating 'Singularity Services'. Naturally Shwaps set a coarse and prayed thanks to that, oh so, merciful deity who obviously had money riding on Shwaps' journey as well.

The station was owned and run by someone with a thick West Country accent but claimed never to have even been to Earth, let alone Cornwall. Upon their landing he ventured out onto the landing pad to greet his new visitors but was greeted back by something not so friendly.

"Where are we? How far did we come?" Shwaps asked quickly, running towards the owner, waving his arms about.

"Most people ask that," said the farmer man calmly, "just not quite in that way," he took a small step back from Shwaps who was practically kissing the man at this point. "You've travelled a good forty thousand light years from the Cluster Hole," he grinned, seemingly having his own private joke about the term 'Cluster Hole', "You boys look like Terrans. Earth ain't no more then a hundred light years from here."

Shwaps and Phil grinned and jumped wildly up and down in delight. "We did it! Who knew it'd be so easy!? We've got rooks of time and Earth is only a hundred light years away!"

Hold on, Lads," interrupted the owner, "I don't want to be a bother but don't forget about the time lag"

"What!?" screamed Phil, "what 'Time Lag'?"

"There's always a time lag when you go through a black hole," the good ole days farmer type replied placidly.

Shwaps glanced at the date on his watch then at a large digital time readout on the side of the building. They were, indeed, different. It turned out that, overall, they had just around six hours to get home. After all of this, just six hours to get back to the four old toffs who had sent him on this insane quest. Transport! Transportation was needed and for some definition of the term 'fair price' it was kindly provided by the owner in the form of 'A Beauty' as the owner had so casually described it. The 'beauty' was actually closer to a 'Clapped Out Old Banger' as Phil had so subtly corrected. Still a ship was a ship and Shwaps wanted his money.

Amazingly enough the banger managed to survive all the way back to Earth but burnt up in the atmosphere after the handbrake was found not to work. To be fair, it was quite a sight as a space hippie noted thusly; "Dude, your car just, like, burnt up in Earths atmosphere, man." Happily enough Phil, in all his intellectual glory managed to find the time to devise a retort in the form of; "Shut up, you stupid little person."

With only fifty three minutes left to spare the two, by now filthy, individuals fell against the ticket desk at Cape Canaveral and with wheezed, dust laden breaths managed to cough "Two to Heathrow" before collapsing altogether.

Again the four old men were sat sipping brandy and telling stories when one of them suddenly looked up, remembering the bet they had made eighty days ago. "Do you realize that in around two minutes that young lad, Gerald, will have to leave and finally pay for everything he's broken," he chortled briefly, "that is if he is still even alive."

"I hope he knows how to write a cheque," said another sarcastically.

The clock began to chime the twelfth hour and, right on que, the door burst open. "Where's my money!?"

The old men were stunned. "Who's he?" exclaimed the oldest pointing at Phil.

"He's the one you have to pay another five grand!"

There was much grumbling from the group of four only to end with that inevitable question, "why?"

"He come with me, went through what I went through. He deserves it!" There was more grumbling from the old men. "I'm willing to leave this club," bribed Shwaps.

Spontaneously the old men stopped grumbling and each dived for there cheque books, only then to compose themselves civilly again. "I assure you, your cheque will be in the post," he smiled sickly and glanced at both of them, "Ehh, both of yours."

"I bloody well hope so!" Shwaps placed a hand on Phil's shoulder, "come on, lets go home," they were about to leave when he suddenly realised something and pointed to the chair he had been sitting in eighty days ago. "Where's my Kebab!?"

Amethyst

With the great sphere hanging so low in the sky it was only now possible to see the array of new stars and obscure constellations the small moon had to offer. The huge Jovian-Class planet laid lethargically on the horizon casting an odd green hue about the surface which shimmered in the thick evening air.

"The evenings here are long," a voice crackled over the radio, "but the days are even longer."

"What about the nights?" the radio hissed back, leaving a strange, intangible echo around the helmet of the spacesuit.

The radio remained silent for a few seconds more, then snapped on again. "None existent," the feminine voice on the other end seemed sombre at the prospect. "Get back ASAP, we still don't know the full extent of the radiation here," she ended quickly, briefing over how truly alien this world was.

"Acknowledged," the radio sounded one last time before clicking off.

There was no sun here, at least none apparent to the small moon in orbit around the vast green giant that crawled slowly across the sky. Majestic as the sight was the planet bathed its tiny partner in a sea of radiation making its celestial beauty all but un-viewable.

As the recon team neared a small cave entrance in the rocky landscape the ground glinted against the planet high in the sky. Minerals in the rock shone and refracted with an intense purple, strange to look at but somehow natural as it transited, shimmering from the otherworldly green layering the thick air.

"Base, we've got something here we should check out," the recon leader crackled again over the radio.

"There's a lot of things we need to check out, Epsilon, but we need you back here," there was a pause and a clatter over the frequency. "Stasis systems are failing already and the encampment isn't up yet, let alone the radiation shield."

The recon leader squinted into the dusky haze and raised some optics to his visor to see a concentration of the purple rocks around the cave entrance. "Copy, but there might be a cave system out here that could temporarily shield the sleepers."

There was static for a moment or two before the radio buzzed back into life. "Understood, Recon Epsilon, investigate the caves to confirm viable protection for our people then immediately return to base."

"Acknowledged, Discovery. Will report progress in one standard hour," the radio clicked off again and the recon leader turned to his two colleagues. "Looks like we're doing some investigating, guys. Harris; I want rock samples and Peterson; keep an eye on those radiation levels. This place might be home for a little while."

"Great..." Peterson mumbled, perturbed and muffled by his helmet, "I always loved caves."

Harris bent down, running her gloved hand over the glowing ground. "I've never seen anything like this," she hovered her hand over the surface, blocking out the planet-light, causing the rocks to loose their luminosity. "They're reacting to the light."

"Or radiation," the recon leader added quietly.

"Speaking of radiation..." Peterson tapped a monitor on the arm of his spacesuit which was acknowledged by his commander, nodding and touching Harris on the arm in order to leave.

As the planet reached ever higher into the sky it obscured the thousand million pinpoints of pure light in the deep black. Its sheer enormous size was capable of blotting out the very sky itself and its deadly radiation able to exterminate all exposed life in seconds. This being the case they decided it was more than a good idea to start moving.

The walk to the cave entrance, although short, was made exhausting from a combination of the moons unusually high gravity and a tidal force from the giant planet that was placing abnormal stresses on the recon teams bodies. By the time they had finally arrived the planet had completed its low roll along the moons horizon. Already it was climbing higher into the dazzlingly starlit sky, the radiation levels rising dramatically as it did.

"Quickly, get inside," the recon leader hurriedly pressed the other two into the entrance and down into the dark tunnels that followed. Before he followed suit he looked back out and over the brilliantly bright dawn mixed with green and purples as the whole surface of the moon came alive with dancing colours as it responded to the growing radiation.

"Alright, we're safe for now," Peterson said quickly, staring at the falling needle on his monitor.

"Phillips!" Harris barked at the recon leader, breathing heavily, "Weren't you supposed to know when planet-rise was?"

"I swear it didn't happen that early yesterday," Phillips tried to gain some limited amount of breath back from the dwindling supply of air in his tank. "Peterson, will this place be safe until the planet sets?"

Peterson looked back at his monitor and gritted his teeth. "Well, it's all academic now, last rise planet exposure was deadly for six standard hours. Not to mention that at this rate we'll have to keep going deeper to escape the radiation, it's already rising here as it is."

Phillips looked back up the tunnel they had come down. "Go any deeper we might not be able to get a radio signal out," he mused to himself. "Discovery...Discovery come in," there was a short pause and a garbled acknowledgement. "Discovery, planet-rise has occurred earlier then expected. These tunnels are providing some protection but we cannot return until radiation levels have reduced. Say again, we are unable to vacate cave system until radiation has subsided."

"...planet...-diation...t-...-el sy..." The radio crackled uncontrollably making the message unintelligible, "unab-...-eam...-main in...-ion...is saf-...-se ou-..."

"Radiation..." Peterson stated simply, "we need to get deeper."

"Agreed," Harris quickly offered while Phillips nodded shallowly.

Without a second thought the team immediately started down the rocky tunnel with an eerie purple glow coating the alien walls. As they dove deeper into the moons crust the glow grew brighter. It grew so much that as the natural surface light grew dim it was quickly replaced by the unsettling hue. Eventually they emerged into a large subterranean cavern with a dark pool at its centre and odd structures hanging from the ceiling. Again the place was lit by the same strange glow as though the walls themselves were tinted floodlights.

"Can you believe this?" breathed Harris, gazing at the distorted reflections in the shimmering pool.

"Hmm..." Peterson failed to acknowledge as he intently watched the monitor on his arm. "I think we should be alright here," he checked the monitor again and waved his arm around in front of him, "but there's still small levels of radiation, unrelated to the surface."

"Is it dangerous?" Phillips asked quickly, turning from the spectacle before them.

Peterson took a few steps towards the pool and crouched down the best he could in his suit. "No. It seems to be this," he reached down to the pool, making the surface frost over before he could touch it. "Caesium," he stated abruptly, pulling his hand back, "the coolant in my suit is causing it to freeze."

Phillips took a step closer and peered into the slick, sliver like pool. "Fascinating, I'm sure, but I'm more concerned about when it's safe to leave."

"Planet exposure will be lethal for at least the next six hours. Discovery is fully aware of this and knows we are at least safe," Peterson paused for a second, considering the best way to make his request. "That in mind I'd like to collect some readings and I suggest we explore this place the best we can."

"Supply camp?" Phillips mused abruptly, looking around at the open cavern.

"At the very least. Discovery hasn't got nearly enough space, especially with everyone waking up," Peterson looked around subtly. "This could be just what we've been looking for."

Phillips thought for a second and looked to a set of openings at the rear of the cavern. "Fine, take your readings, I'll check out the rest of this place," he turned and found Harris examining the glowing cave walls. "Harris, you're with me," he stepped closer, reaching out a hand to her, "Harris."

"This can't be," she murmured to herself, twisting awkwardly in her suit to face Phillips, "it's like there are living veins in the wall itself."

"Organic?" questioned Phillips, looking closely at the surface. Embedded into the wall there did, indeed, appear to be veins that pulsed a glowing fluid through the solid rock. "What the..."

"Bio-luminescent fluids," Harris started, "possibly some form of nutrient transport," she stood back and looked intently at the throbbing wall, focusing on a strange cluster of small grass like fibres which some of the veins centralised around. "These appear to be some form of cilium; a means to filter feed or absorb nutrients. What could it possibly be absorbing?"

"The radiation?" Peterson offered, "as a energy source to fix atmospheric chemicals," he finished, not even turning away from what he was doing.

Harris raised her eyebrows, her mouth hanging open. "It's not unheard of. Radiosynthesis in Fungi back on Earth using Melanin instead of Chlorophyll," she considered the idea for a few more seconds. "Question is; where is it being directed?"

Phillips looked around again, concluding the directionality of the fluids. "Let's find out then," he pointed to one of the rear openings that the veins appeared to travel down. "Peterson, I want contact every twenty minutes." Peterson nodded shallowly as he continued to work, barely even aware he had been addressed with the other two heading off towards the tunnel.

After several minutes of walking Phillips and Harris came to another, much smaller cavern. This had two other exits and a much higher concentration of veins, coalescing into several large, vertically elongate polyps on the ground. Each throbbed like the veins and seemed to sway gently against a breeze that didn't exist.

Harris knelt down to one of the polyps to inspect it. "This is new," she said, stretching out an arm to it, mesmerised.

"Careful," Phillips snapped, "we've got no idea what these things are or if they could be dangerous."

"I severely doubt that," she brushed away some loose sand from its base to find a tubule seeming to connect each of the polyps. As she did the growth began to split along the sides, its outer layers peeling back slowly to expose a fleshy, stem like structure wrapped in the pulsating veins. "This is incredible. I never could have believed we'd find something like this," she scrutinized the structure, causing Phillips to shift uneasily. "I don't think this is floral. The closest thing I could say it resembles is terran Hemichordate, possibly Pterobranchia, but with it being completely alien I couldn't even begin to speculate."

Phillips pulled her up from the swaying polyp. "In English, doctor."

"It's technically animalia," she started, turning around, "possibly one huge colonial creature throughout these tunnels. The fibrous growths on the surface and in the cavern absorbing radiation to metabolize with," she looked back at the eerie sack of flesh as it seemed to lean towards her slightly. "As for this thing...Could be some type of Zooid, a single living organism within the greater colony," despite Phillips' encouragement against going near the creature Harris, again, knelt back down beside it. As she did the veins began to unwrap from the central stalk, allowing a collection of short tentacles to peel away from it, wavering in the air as if it were water. "This is fascinating, I need to take a specimen."

"Harris-" Phillips tried unsuccessfully.

"I know the risks but this is possibly the most complex extra-solar organism ever discovered. We can bring a team back later, yes, but the sooner I get this under the microscope-" she was cut off by Phillips raising his hands and nodding quickly.

"Fine, just try not to hurt it."

Harris smiled briefly and set to retrieving a small surgical knife from her field kit. " Of course not, I'm sure it won't miss one of these stalks," she moved in towards the creature with the knife in hand forcing the tentacles to recoil away from her as if they knew what was coming. She carefully managed to maneuver her blade against the base of the stalk and cleanly slice free a tentacle. As soon as she did though, the polyps skin snapped shut, barely allowing Harris to free her hand. With this the purple glow illuminating the site abruptly ceased, leaving them in complete pitch blackness.

"Lamps," Phillips addressed subtly in the overwhelming darkness.

"Don't have to tell me twice," Harris murmured uneasily, scrambling to find the switch to her headlamp. Finally she grazed across it causing a momentarily blinding burst of light before her eyes adjusted to see a deadly still, black polyp. She sighed and turned around where her light met a ghostly skeletal face, tinted a sickly green as it darted across her vision creating a sheer panic that forced her to scream. Then, as quickly as it had appeared, it was replaced with Phillips' visored features.

"What's wrong?" Phillips said quickly, stretching a hand out to help her up.

She snapped her head from side to side, desperately trying to illuminate the cave walls with the meagre beam of her headlamp. "Did you-" she considered what she had seen, or if she had, in fact, seen anything at all. "It was...A shock. Losing the light like that...I..." she stuttered, trying to make sense of what was happening, "my eyes were playing tricks on me."

"It's alright," Phillips said reassuringly, "we're trapped in an alien cave network on a world parsecs away from home, its natural to be a bit jitterish." He tapped the dull, flickering light on his helmet. "Especially when your damn lamp won't work."

Harris looked around again nervously, the flickered shadows catching her eye uneasily. "Maybe we should head back."

Phillips nodded, reaching for his radio. "Peterson, we're on our way back," he stated clearly only to be met with a steady static. "Peterson, respond," still there was nothing but the grating drone. "Report your situation. Have the-" the radio blasted static again for a second before abruptly stopping leaving the two in a deadly silence. For several long seconds there was nothing as they looked at each other in the unnervingly low light.

"Maybe it's the radia-" Harris tried, only to be cut off by Phillips' radio again. It blasted a stunted, rhythmic timbre that dipped in pitch with each passing sequence of repeated tones. Its frequency whipped from squeals to rumbling growls, continuingly stamping out the eerily irregular rhythm until it abruptly stopped. It now left the dark cavern in an absolute silence that was no better then the chaotic din that had preceded.

"Phillips!" the radio garbled at last causing Phillips and Harris to start back, "where the hell have you been? I can't see a damn thing."

Phillips tentatively reached for his radio again, unsure whether he should risk using it again. "Peterson?" he said cautiously, deciding take the chance, "we've..." he considered giving him a full appraisal of the situation but knew brief contact was probably better, "we've got some issues, heading back now," he tentatively released the radio, allowing the faint crackle of the open channel to fall silent. "Come on," Phillips gestured to Harris encouraging her to take the lead back down the tunnel they had originally entered through.

As they walked further back towards the first cavern it became apparent that the blackout had occurred throughout the network of tunnels, leaving the entire labyrinth in a dense, sickly blackness.

"Peterson can't be happy being left alone in this," Harris murmured after several minutes, trying to reassure herself against the desolate silence and dark.

"I am sure he is not," came Phillips' voice, still and without concern. Then it was silent once again, nothing to break the stillness but their footsteps crunching on the alien gravel.

Eventually the narrow tunnel opened back out into the main cavern where Harris darted forward, glancing around, spilling small pools of light about the ground. "He's gone," she spurted out, swinging around having caught no sight of Peterson.

Phillips stared straight forwards, un-phased by the fact one of his team had disappeared. "Indeed he is," he flicked his glazed eyes to Harris, "but he is safe...For now."

"Phillips..." Harris mouthed subtly, unsure of what was taking place.

"Phillips is here...He merely...facilitates our presence here," as he finished speaking the air around him shifted as another of the ghostly skulls jumped from Phillips' helmet. It streaked around him for a second before blurring back, leaving a faint green haze in the air.

"You're sentient..." Harris considered, too intrigued to be terrified. "Please, don't hurt them."

The creature inhabiting Phillips snapped its attention back to Harris, having been distracted by the design of body. "You hurt us," it said sternly, "we felt your presence and welcomed you...You hurt us."

Harris tightened her grip on the sample container housing the specimen of the alien being. "We didn't know, we thought you were-"

"Lesser?" the being finished, clearly displeased with human rationale, "we learn much from this body but not that all is equal in your eyes."

"I'm sorry, I truly am," she raised the sample container, offering it before placing it on the ground in front of Phillips. "Please, let him go."

The being turned its gaze quickly to the container and produced a low hissing sound as its true self shifted into the open air once again. This time instead of withdrawing it darted around Phillips' helmet, the hissing changing into an off key whine, shifting in pitch and forming a rhythm much like that produced by the radio. With the tempo like whine growing in intensity several more eerie green skeletal figures raced into vision causing the fear to finally overwhelm Harris' inquisitive nature. They hovered around Phillips, each momentarily blurring into each other, dragging the being of one another across the thick air. Harris tried to step back, only to realise that these strange ethereal creatures were all around her, boxing her against Phillips.

"Please..." she tried again, her voice weak and trembling, tears beginning to form in the corner of her eyes, "please," she mouthed one last time as a tear finally broke loose and streaked down her cheek.

"Ours is not yours," the creature inside Phillips stated firmly as the veins about the walls began to faintly pulse again, affording the cavern with an uncomfortable illumination. "Our body is weak..." with the light level rising again it slowly became clear that there were dozens more of the aliens all around, each now with a faint, skeletal body. Their arms fell to their reverse jointed knees with three long, gripping fingers on each hand. A rib dominated torso made up their upper body leading to a long, thin neck that afforded little support for the heads that drifted around on the tenticular vertebrae. "Our mind is strong," it continued, "you harm our body...we will take your mind..."

Harris whimpered as the ever growing presence of the creatures around her moved closer "...No..." she murmured, the tears now streaming down her face as one of the ethereal beings reached forward its bony arm towards her, clasping its long, slender fingers as it went.

"One must remain..." the creature inside Phillips said finally before Harris was taken, "so that no more return."

Several hours later a slow, distant clicking drifted through a dreamless void approaching closer then falling away again. It swung back and forth for some time until it took a place in the real world, gradually awakening Peterson from a disturbing slumber. He opened his eyes slightly and caught a glimpse of the moons surface, the planet now low in the sky and the intense field of purple fading away. He managed to move his arm to see that it was the radiation monitor that had been clicking so readily. The needle was high but not so high that the dose he was receiving was fatal. Suddenly his radio blasted, making him start up, looking around and finding that he was at the mouth of the cave. The radio blasted again, this time causing him to answer it.

"Peterson," he answered weakly.

"What happened? You've been out of contact for hours," the commanders voice crackled, "are you all ok?"

He looked around to find he was alone. Then it all came back to him. The creatures, their minds, so free and powerful but their brains so fragile, housed in those polyp like structures. They had show him everything and kept the others as a warning. "I...I'm all that's left..."

"What is that supposed to mean?" the radio demanded.

Peterson thought for a second, trying to comprehend all that he had gone through and could only manage one simple statement. "We're not alone."

Within

"L'enfer, c'est les autres" (Hell is other people)

– Jean-Paul Satre

With an echoed slam the hydraulics sealed shut. It shuddered the entire shelter, rattling objects from shelves and wits from people. We were trapped. Trapped in a cage of our own design and, at last, we were safe.

That was four months ago. Of course it could have been weeks or months. It could have even been years. There are no clocks here, no calendars, nothing to remind us of the outside. 'Detrimental to the collective psyche,' they told us, 'better for everyone this way,' they told us. I'll tell you what's detrimental to the collective psyche; rotten, stinking bread and a three by six cell. But the water, oh, that deadly sweet water.

Bose drank himself up enough to slit ear to ear in the first week. Or was it month? I don't remember.

Now the water look all pretty, don't you think? Pretty in pink and tasting funny, but I don't drink it. My old Nein told me don't never drink nothing that tastes funny. I found the rain leaks, though, fresh and bland like it should be. Harry calls me stupid, Lily calls me dumb. They like the pretty water, they say it makes them feel good,

29

makes them relax, makes them fun, but I'm not fun. I tried some a while back but I think it turned me strange. Nein told me the funny water would make me strange. At least I know why we're in here, the others forgot, forgot about that what happened outside. Or I thought I remembered. I might've never knew. That's it, I never did know what happened outside, but neither did anyone else. If we did we'd be like Bose. Instead we're in here because of it. Sometimes I think they know, know what happened. I hear screams when they're sleeping, mumbled words when they're alone. The others don't hear but I do, I do and so does Anne.

"You're still here, aren't you?" she says to me, "you're not gone like the others?" She don't like the pretty water neither, only she never did. Always from the fresh falling she drank. She must have listened to her Nein more than me. "Don't trust the others. Never trust the others. Their going out of their minds." Harry called her stupid too, just because she wanted to know what happened to the outside. But I wanted to know too, so I helped her.

"What happened?" I asked her, "what happened to the others? What happened to me?"

She didn't trust that I could keep secrets but she told me anyway. "I don't know why they would do it but they sent us in here with the hope of surviving, only to die because of that damned water. They didn't want us to know what's out there. They just wanted us to die quietly in here."

I didn't see no meaning to that. No meaning to dying for nothing. "I ain't wanting to die. I don't wanna be no fountain like Bose!"

Anne looked all queer at me, like I wasn't me. "That stuff really messes you up, doesn't it? How much did you have?" I don't understand not half of what she says but I liked she didn't call me stupid. "The water, how much did you drink?"

"I ain't drunk much. Few glasses most, then you showed me fresh falling."

"Fast acting. It might wear off but-" she ain't never said nothing outright that scared me but I know she thinks the bad things. The bad things for me, the bad things for her. "I need to get to the cistern, take a look at the filtration system. I'm sure I can figure something out, stop things from getting any worse at the very least."

I still never figured what she was saying but it was good, for the good of us. "Most of them are down there, though, drinking themselves to death." Anne never asked what she didn't need but I never liked when she did any more. "I need a distraction, just get them away from the cistern for a few minutes-"

"Minutes ain't meaning nothing no more."

"Please, just a little bit. Do you understand?" I got her meaning one time. I ain't liking it but she smiled nice when I nodded.

"Good, just don't annoy them. I'm not overly sure of what they might be capable of."

The tank weren't no place I wanted to be. Cold, wet, stinking all foul. Ain't no place to sleep either. No place to sleep for so many, not all cut up and slit. Maybe they had a party? All decorated in bright red, streamers and piñatas. I never liked no parties like this one.

"My god, what have they done to each other?" Anne didn't like it no less than me, she couldn't hold her eats.

"I like my parts together."

"I always liked everything on the inside too," she looked all sad at me, ain't nothing wrong with being sad. "I still need you to go in there, just a distraction, nothing more. I'll go round the back but don't let them see me..." I wanted a smile so I nodded again and she left. Weren't no one left at the party but Harry, Lily and Wes. Wes looked though he were falling sleep. Ain't no point waking someone, not when he be needing rest to get those arms back.

"Hey, Harry...Lily," I never been much more scared than that, all scared they ain't liking me.

"Stupid!" I ain't stupid, they're stupid, "stupid! stupid! stupid!" I know I ain't 'cos Anne says so and I be helping her over there.

"I don't want no nasty, jus' wanna talk," I don't get what Anne be doing but she doing good, I think.

"Talk 'bout you bein' dumb!" don't like Lily, "talk 'bout you bein' stupid!"

I ain't stupid. "You had a party?" Anne gonna be done soon.

"Stupid! Stupid! Stupid!"

As I saw that spanner fall, slipping through Annes grip I had a moment of pure clarity. I saw the horror around me, the twisted, scarred faces of those before me, the state of my own hands, filthy, scratched and bloodied. Then I heard the clang as the spanner bounced on the ground and my mind fell away again.

"Wha'!" Harry didn't like no one crashing his party. He didn't like no one, specially if it was Anne. I never seen no one move like that before, pushing her down. I never liked no screaming. It got changed when he pushed down on her neck. Don't like no gargle scream, ain't not a sound I want to hear again. I don't know what gotta happen. He got to stop, that's what gotta happen. I gotta make him stop. Sharps in their hands make them sleep. I gotta guess sharp make him sleep too. Quiet sharp through the air, sleeping, sleeping, got to rest. Such a pretty fountain, just like Bose. Anne ain't not happy, though, she looking all scared like I'm not me. 'For another time', she'd says, when Lily ran away.

"It's ok..." Anne look like she more scared of the quiet sharp than me. Didn't like it anyway so I threw it away. "Whatever's in the water must be progressive, you're getting worse." I not liking 'getting worse,' ain't nothing like what it should be. Blurry, dreamy, cloudy eyes. "What just happened is for another time, though. I don't care what's out there, we need to escape. She'll only go and tell the others then we'll end up like the rest of these poor souls."

"I like out," not a thought, not a pause, I know what I want.

"That freshwater leak has got to come from somewhere, I'm going to find out where," Anne thought we would sleep soon, like the others. She didn't like sleeping. My old Nein went to sleep once. I waited but she never woke up. Then we were at fresh falling, I ain't knowing how, blurred eyes made me forget. I think I should sleep soon.

"I knew it!" I liked when Anne was happy, "there is a way out up there, straight to the surface. Hide yourself and wait for me. I'll find safety and come back for you. God willing, I think you're not beyond saving."

Now I'm alone. I waited for her, did just what she said. Hid behind wooden slits, in the musty cloth. She's still not come for me. I used to see the others stumble by. I don't see anything now, one fell to me, sleeping. They all sleep now and it's time I did too. Hazy, blurry sleep before my eyes, I'm going away.

"No life..."

Eyes open, dark all round. I don't like dark, dark is scary, dark is bad.

"No life anywhere..."

"Anne?" I thought I were sleeping, not a people all around. Pretty water put them all down. Endless time put out the lights.

"Life..."

I fell out the wooden slits, Anne's voice leading, legs don't work no more. Peoples sleeping, sleeping all around but she's still there. That voice in the dark.

"Life everywhere...Lights in the dark."

I ain't liking Anne no more. She never scared me like this before.

"Swirling vortex, harrowed skies. Tall as trees, leathered skin. Reaching into the bloodied clouds, impaling spire...Listen..."

I listened. I saw. Eyes like lights in the dark, blurred and moving, tall and pulsed, veins of void. Creeping fingers, touching, touching all, learning, learning me.

Anne's voice failing, it faulted at the last. "They're in..."

In or out, it matters not. My mind is lost and it's time to sleep. Motion carries me, carries me far away, far to solace and safety. I am here but I am gone. A mind so poisoned, poisoned by self, those who we fled take me home. Finally I hear in whispered voice, in wheezing air. Learnt of us they came, knew of us they spoke, "Harm.   No   Harm."

The Messenger

The Messengers. Not the most glamorous, influential or even well known of castes. Their task was, for the best part, simple; act as go betweens for people and city governments. Whether that meant delivering messages, packages or anything else that needed to get from one place to another. Despite being an indispensable role in the day to day running of civilization, they tended to go by all but unnoticed. To their advantage, this meant that their work was generally unhindered, but it also meant that it was, too, unappreciated. Not to say there was nothing to appreciate about The Messengers, they were only the fastest, most agile runners in the known world. This was not an easy reputation to gain, either, especially with the trade routes expanding, as they were, and the demand for fast communication growing.

Cydonia had been trying for years to capitalize on this, mainly by publicizing their own version of The Messengers. Still, Tyn Tychus, 'The Golden State' as it was known, continued to hold the unwavering monopoly on these routes. This was considered by some to be down to the fact that, where Cydonia wasted time promoting their runners, Tyn Tychus ignored The Messengers all together, allowing them to get on with their work no matter what. Soon, none of this was to matter, though, not with the cataclysm and the coming of the scourge. In time there would be nothing but that one lone, unknown Messenger facing the end, only to stand up and defy it.

Not much was known about the cataclysm, vague stories from travellers told of a hole in the Earth. Fire, brimstone and the clatter of a thousand metallic limbs. Drunken tales from the tongue of Barbarous, the lying scorn, no doubt. Then, one day, caravans out of Cealaphon stopped. Had they finally given into Cydonias false charm and shoddy goods? Of course the Cydonians denied it all, as usual, offending the Tychus parliament with their blazoned attitude. With the political back and forth the change went almost completely unnoticed. The change in the sky and an eerie rumble growing on the air. A deep, blood red had replaced the soft orange of dusk lately as well as a thick, black veil hanging low on the horizon, its size doubling with each passing day. Then on one quiet, unassuming evening, it arrived.

The Messenger sat silently at his usual back table, clutching a wrapped parcel with one hand and a tankard of mead with the other. The package its self wasn't overly interesting nor important, some simple trinkets sent by a desperate relative in an attempt to end a family feud. Judging by the reaction of the recipient, who had promptly refused to accept the delivery, the attempt had clearly failed. It was late now and pointless returning the item to its sender until morning so the only thing left to do was to grab a few quiet drinks before returning to the dorm. For years this had been the general idea of things in the consideration of most Messengers, although, it rarely ever went to plan. That night was going to be no exception either, only it wasn't going to be the exception in the most spectacular way.

The burly bartender started strolling towards the corner table and The Messenger pulled the package back towards him knowing, as he did, the tendency for theft in these parts. The tender bunched up a damp dish cloth in his large, stubby hands and threw it on the table before leaning on his hairy knuckles, forcing a whimpered creek from the table.

"Busy night, son?" the tender growled from a set of huge, yellow teeth.

The Messenger took a subtle swig from the tankard and placed it gently back on the table. "Could say that," he knew what was coming, this was far from the first time it had ever happened. The city's bars weren't overly keen on Messengers frequenting their premises. It had something to with 'shifty hands and agile bands.' An old barkeep saying about Messengers habit of running out without paying. Only fair, really, considering how bars were the typical place where Messengers deliveries went missing.

"Hope you've got coin, boy. I'd hate for there to be trouble," the tender glanced down the parcel and cracked a grin.

"I'm thinking that wouldn't be any good for either of us," he snatched a look at the door, then back at the large barkeep in front of him. Typically whatever form of theft occurred all depended on who acted first and tonight it wasn't looking good for The Messenger, especially seeing as how two bouncers had silently positioned themselves either side of the doorway. At this point The Messenger might as well have simply handed over the package along with the right change and been on his way. Of course, on that night, no one expected a fireball to crash through the bars roof. Considering that this is exactly what happened, The Messenger felt as though he should exploit the situation to the best of his ability and, in the ensuing chaos, ran. As the buildings wooden beams quickly caught alight around him, he dived over a table, managing to finish off his tankard as he glided across its surface. In another smooth movement he landed and twisted past the bouncers, who were now much too preoccupied with the collapsing masonry all around them.

Outside he was presented with a deafening roar as dozens more fireballs arced through the sky, drawing thick black streaks behind them. The Messenger stumbled backwards up the cobble street, watching, unbelieving as the sky seemed to fall towards him. Around him people were running and screaming. Some were carrying various personal belongings in their arms, others just trying to get away. So many questions were racing through peoples minds. What was happening? How was it happening? Tychun defences were the best on the continent. Nothing had breached the walls in over seven hundred years, nothing had ever been able to bypass the cannons which had so far, tonight, remained silent. Suddenly everything stopped, the people in the streets froze and turned towards the oncoming assault. The black smoke had started to spill over the walls, obscuring everything that it touched. From beyond there was a strange clattering and a tremor that rumbled through the ground. Unknown to most who were now transfixed on the cloud creeping into the city, the fireballs raining from beyond the smoke had stopped, leaving the districts to burn. Then something was there, something moving beyond the black veil. Slowly a huge metallic limb unfolded over the wall and fell down into the city, its pointed tip crushing some poor souls home below. It heaved at its joints as if it was about to haul the rest of its bulk over the wall and the silhouette of another leg pressed against the layer of smoke. Without notice there were several enormous blasts from the citadel at the centre of the city as the powerful cannons abruptly came to life. Explosions beyond the veil briefly illuminated a vast metal body with clawed arms grasping at the ramparts. More explosions tore through the metal creatures leg, ripping the beasts appendage away from its body. It forced the unbalanced bulk to withdraw behind its smokescreen, leaving the leg to crash down across the market district. As its imposing shape faded into the black a deafening cheer went up from the entire city only to be quickly silenced by a harrowing, tubular roar from beyond the walls. Again the flames began raining, forcing those rejoicing in the streets to take to their heels once more. This time The Messenger went along with them, fleeing towards the Citadel, only for a much different reason then the others. They sought protection, he sought answers. The captain of the city militia had assured him weeks ago that the black veil hanging on the horizon was nothing to be concerned about. He had his doubts about what he had been told then but had learnt not to question the militia if a stint in the stocks wanted to be avoided.

After running with the crowd for several minutes he peeled off and slipped into an otherwise hidden drainage pipe at the foot of the vast citadel fortifications. The city was old and the streets were complicated but The Messengers knew all the short cuts, even those that weren't strictly supposed to exist. He quickly shuffled through the damp tunnels with the sound of outside explosions echoing through the concrete. The pipes twisted and turned, each leading to various points all over the city. If not for an intimate knowledge of this labyrinth he could of become lost down there for days, in fact, in the past he had. Luckily it wasn't long before he came to a grate leading to the inner sanctum, the most protected area in the whole citadel. It was a large, well stocked chamber which was to serve as protection for the city's people in times of need. Rather than being filled with desperate civilians, though, it was empty bar the Militia Captain and the City Regent, leader of the province, standing either side of an unusual pedestal, bickering in hushed tones. Soon they were joined by a third individual who The Messenger did not recognize. The new person was adorned in a long robe with a strange looking pointed hat, its wide rim partially obscuring his face.

"Do you have it?" the Captain started, agitatedly stepping forward.

"I am afraid I do not," the robed man tilted his head to reveal a lengthy grey beard tucked into his cloak.

The Regent calmly sidled in front of the Captain and put up her hand before he could have an outburst. "We were assured its use when the time came," she reached up to her head and pulled her tiara away, making sure none of her bright blonde hair fell aside, "your people were to be greatly rewarded," she offered up the tiara before lowering it.

"Come to that you told us they wouldn't come yet," the Captain growled from behind the Regent, not able to control himself.

"An oversight. After all, how damaging could a menace of your own creation be?" his tone was immersed in condescension and a faint smirk appeared under the rim of his hat, "it won't happen again."

"So the Heart?" The Regent enquired more forcefully this time, running a hand over a hollow atop the pedestal.

"Rest in mind that it is complete, the power has been bound and efforts are being made to retrieve the item. I have already dispatched my apprentice for Indra..."

The Messenger mouthed the name 'Indra' like it was familiar. Supposedly it was an old fort overtaken by Mancers and Mystics who experimented in the arcane arts.

"Be sure your *efforts* succeed, mage," The Captain stated firmly, gritting his teeth, "that Heart is the only thing standing between us and annihilation. Just remember that means you as well!"

The mage bowed his head and turned to leave calmly but hesitated before moving towards the door. "I must commend you on your creations. They are most elaborately horrific. Your city will not last and it is doubtful that even my apprentice will make it in time," he paused and glanced back over his shoulder at the two uneasy leaders, "but there is always hope," he smirked again and began walking briskly towards the door, leaving The Regent and The Captain to, again, bicker fruitlessly.

"Indra," The Messenger whispered as a demented idea began to form in his head. Plenty of people knew where Indra was but none ever dared approach it, afraid of what lay inside. He started away from the grate, heading back down the tunnel, considering the insane plan. The Indrans were clearly a reclusive group with no idea of the outside world so he knew the Mages' Apprentice would never make it in time. By the time he returned with The Heart, whatever it was, Tyn Tychus would be just a ruin. It needed to be retrieved by someone who knew the country, who was fast and who cared about the city enough to actually do it. It needed a Messenger. By the time this had passed through his mind The Messenger was already nearing one of the waste tunnels out of the city. Luckily they were well hidden so it was unlikely whatever was out there would find them and even if they did they would likely be lost in the tunnel network for weeks. As he approached the end he could see the black mist drifting in from outside. Against it was the eerie orange hue of flames and shimmers of movement. Unthinking, he darted from the tunnel into the tall swamp grass that concealed the entrance. Without looking around he moved as fast as he could through the boggy reeds until stumbling over onto more solid ground. It was only now that he looked up and around. The dense mist obscured most of his view but high up in it moved the silhouette of a huge bulk heading towards the city, another of those abominations trying to breach the wall. The Messenger continued to lay rigid as it began to pass over him, unaware of his presence. The massive metal legs stamped down on either side of him as it passed. Six enormous claws driving down, in succession, into the ground. As it moved away, The Messenger quickly got back to his feet and raced through the black veil once more, knowing it could not go on forever.

As he ran, he passed several more of the metallic monstrosities, some smaller then the first, some even of completely different shape, apparently designed for varying purposes. Rather than ponder on this The Messenger considered they were all utilized to the same end. Instead he continued on until he saw moonlight piercing through the fog, illuminating the steep, far side of the valley that housed Tychus. Still refusing to stop he attacked the hill head on and managed to get half way up before slowing. Eventually he clawed his way to the top and partially collapsed in front of a thick tree line. He breathed heavily for a few seconds before pressing himself up again and looking back at the valley under siege.

The very tops of those automatons breached the mist, which now laid in the valley like a dark lake, gleaming against the moonlight. Occasionally a fireball roared up from one of them and crashed back down into the city. The Messenger knew he had to get to Indra. He knew the Mages apprentice would never have made it, especially not through Gallowtrees. He slowly turned and looked at the tree line and the dark wood beyond. It was possible to go around but the wood stretched for miles each way, Tychus would definitely be lost before he was even halfway round. Gallowtrees housed the entrance to the Glintstone Caverns, though, which cut straight to the Indra plains. He glanced back at the valley, at his home being overrun with god only knew what, and decided it was the only way. He took another deep breath in, knowing what lay inside, and stepped into the damp black.

The Messenger pushed deep into the wood, past the waxy shrubs, the hanging vines but he could still hear the explosions and ominous crashes from the siege on the city, muffled now by the dense foliage. His gut told him to head back now, before it was too late. Maybe he would be able to do something, help the militia, lead civilians to safety. All of these thoughts were soon silenced by his head telling him that to go back would mean certain death. Besides, there was an inexorable curiosity about the whole situation. The Regent, the Mage. The Heart wasn't just some last hope of the desperate, it was all part of something that had all been planned for far longer than anyone knew. Not just a hope but an answer, an answer to the destruction befalling Tychus and all that would come to the world if the city fell.

The wood scratched at his senses, everything about it was overpowering. The contrast of the bright leaves against the rotting wood, the low drone of hidden creatures around him, the dense air filling his lungs with a warm, sticky moisture. Stories told that people went missing in here, not just lost; every sense of their being got sucked away by the oppressiveness of the wood. At least that's what had happened to the few who managed to escape. As for the rest... Well, it was probably for the best not to consider their fate too closely. Even so, The Messenger couldn't help but think about them, and everything he had been told about not going too far beyond the tree line. If not for the fact that the entrance to Glintstone would have been barely a ten minute walk over good terrain, he would have probably turned around by now. Still, this was far from good terrain. The ground was soft and marshy, the jagged leaves snagging at his clothes and fallen trees constantly blocked his way. Even worse were the numerous vines hanging down from the canopy high overhead. Their prickled skin constantly caught against him, hooked tips grabbing at his arms and legs. Anyone would have thought they were doing it deliberately.

Suddenly he stopped with a horrifying realization, swinging around to catch several vines silently snake back into the undergrowth. He had always wondered why it was called Gallowtrees when, to his knowledge, no-one had ever been deliberately hung here. He briefly chuckled at the blatant, yet so easily overlooked, obviousness of name and promptly felt all hope of living through the next few minutes drain away. Without a second thought of his impending death he set about trying to avoid it by running as fast as he possibly could deeper into the carnivorous forest towards Glintstone. After him struck the vines again, jumping as if fired from the bushes before slithering faster than should be logically possible across the muddy ground. As he ran, diving over debris and swinging across pools, The Messenger thought he could hear a voice screaming in the distance. After several more seconds it became clear that it wasn't actually some part of his mind crying out in terror and that someone else was trapped in here. As he continued to flee the sentient flora, the screaming became louder and less muffled by the dense shrubbery. Then it was abruptly silenced by an even louder, earth shaking screech that was pitched at exactly the right tone to inflict crippling terror on whatever happened to hear it. It made the woods heavy leaves whip around as if there was some terrible wind accompanying the screech and forced The Messenger to a static halt, uncaring what terribleness struck after him. To his surprise, though, there was nothing. Not even the slightest hint of death or the idea that death might be in some way imminent, as it had been for the past few minutes. Instead there was just the deeply unsettling feeling that whatever was ahead was bad enough to scare away everything else that had seemed so bad before.

For a moment there was silence and then a rustling ahead. Whatever made that terrible sound lay just beyond the next veil of bushes, moving around an apparent clearing which, The Messenger feared, would hold the cave entrance. As if he was being compelled by the hand of a god, or a considerably lucrative wager, he moved forward again, slowly this time, and peered through to the clearing.

Lo and behold, there was the entrance to Glintstone Caverns. It was a raised mound of rocks that certainly did its name justice, made up mostly of luminous minerals and shining micas. Impressive as it was, The Messengers immediate attention was, instead, focused on what happened to be moving around in front of it. The sight of it was virtually indescribable, with the stench even worse still. The creature was at least nine feet tall, mostly green, (although this was unlikely to be its natural colouring, having apparently cultured a full body fungus colony) and had inexplicable tendrils rooting it to the ground immediately around it. As it moved the tendrils ripped apart, making the creature groan, before more shot out of its body, lashing themselves to anything they touched. The whole being appeared to be some sort of living combination of earth and trees with no discernable head or limbs, only a huge mass that moved and felt using those fleshy tendrils. It stopped for a moment and let out another piercing screech, again making anything around it try its hardest to flee.

When the creature moved away again The Messenger was able to see an odd looking sack tossed to the side of the caverns entrance. It looked to be made up of leaves and roots, held together by a sticky, fibrous mucus. Unlike the creature, the sack did appear to have a head and at least three visible limbs, bound and mostly obscured by the mess covering them. It would seem as though this is where the initial screaming had originated, probably another soul fleeing Tychus, meeting a less than desirable fate in this place. Just then The Messenger saw something else, something caught up in the binding. It was a hat, just like that of the Mage back in the Citadel. Apparently the Apprentice hadn't heard the stories of Gallowtrees, wandering in here in search of a quick way to Indra. Then again, The Messenger had heard plenty of stories and still entered for exactly the same reason. He thought for a few seconds as the creature dragged its hulk to inspect some soon to be doomed animal. Cooperation wasn't The Messengers strongest suit, or that of any other Messenger for that matter, although the Apprentice would have been able to answer several hundred questions that had began to swell in his mind.

Before he could consider any longer his legs leapt forward, flinging him out of cover and into a full sprint across the clearing. Sliding across wet dirt, he grabbed the cocooned body of the Apprentice and dragged him behind a pile of Glintstones. He hurriedly pulled away the binding from the Apprentices face and looked over the rocks to the caves entrance as the creature began to move back, seemingly chewing on that unfortunate animal. The Messenger turned back to the Apprentice and started to desperately pull at the rest of the cocoon, making him groan as the humid air touched his face.

"Cave?" The Apprentice managed, trying to focus.

"Shh!" The Messenger clamped a hand over The Apprentices mouth as the huge creature loomed overhead, tendrils striking down all around them. For a few seconds it hung in the air as smaller tentacles felt around the ground curiously. Eventually it moved off, ripping up the ground, having apparently not noticed the two interlopers.

"That..." The Apprentice lucidly muffled, through The Messengers fingers, only to have them forced even tighter around his mouth.

"I said be quiet," growled The Messenger, looking at the piles of sparkling rocks around him. "I have an idea," he ripped his hand away from The Apprentices mouth, allowing him to pull away his remaining bonds. "There's another reason why they call it Glintstone Caverns..." he grabbed a few loose rock from the pile and gently knocked two together causing them to spark and briefly ignite a small, green flame. He grinned and tore a length of cloth from his tunic, wrapping it around one of the larger, brighter rocks tightly. He grinned again and picked up the two small rocks before looking up at the bewildered Apprentice. "Cover your ears," he whispered and struck the rocks, allowing the flame to drop onto the cloth, igniting it quickly. Without pause he scooped up the rock, as the fuse burnt down, and threw it as hard as he could at, what he assumed, to be the area of the creatures head. The rock buried its self in the moss covered skin of the, now, angered creature which once more roared at the pair before promptly exploding into a shower of fungus.

"Oh my god!" The Apprentice shouted, getting up unsteadily from the ground, "did you just...? I can't believe..." he sighed, at a loss for any more words as The Messenger quickly moved towards the cave entrance. "Who are you?"

"Lunch for something else in here, just like you, if we don't move," he pointed at the edge of the clearing where the trees were already starting to rustle ominously.

The Apprentice opened his mouth to speak but looked around and decided leaving was probably for the best.

Glintstone Caverns were as beautiful as they were dangerous, being named not only for the obvious reasons but also because their intermittent detonations caused a wondrous glint on the horizon of far away settlements. Of course, they were devoid of any form of life bar Rock Worms and the odd lost rat, the incendiary nature of the caves making them unappealing for long term residence. Even so, Inaran settlers had, long ago, followed the veins of stone deep into the border mountains creating shortcuts through the natural land barriers. This was long before Gallowtrees became the overgrown death trap it was today, though, longer still before Tychus grew into a thriving metropolis.

"Going to tell me who you are, now?" The Apprentice asked, trying to keep up with The Messenger. "Why are you even out here?"

"I'm no one, just a Messenger from the city," he stopped briefly and looked back at his new companion, "and I'm out here for the same reason you are," The Apprentice looked back sideways, bemused by the comment, "only I'm succeeding," he started walking again, quickly passing through the dull pools of light produced by the glowing crystals in the walls.

"The Heart? Who sent you? My master told me I was the only one," The Apprentice now started to lightly jog to keep up with The Messenger.

"I sent myself," he stopped again, this time in front of a fork in the tunnels, and paused for a while. "This Heart can really save the city?"

The Apprentice nodded firmly. "So long as I get it back in time."

"You?" The Messenger asked forcefully, "you'd be dead without me. Now I think you should just leave it to me," he went to move but a hand on his shoulder stopped him.

"Fine, yes, but you need me too. Do you know what the Heart is?" he stared at The Messenger who said nothing, "how do you expect to get to Indra? Get the Heart? Do you even know the way out of here?"

The Messenger eventually nodded, acceptingly. "Fine, I need what you know, but it's my city! I'm not letting any two bit mage slow me down!"

"And I'll try not to take that personally," The Apprentice murmured as The Messenger tried to set off down one of the tunnels again, only to be stopped once more. "We go down there, by the way," The Apprentice added, pointing loosely to the other tunnel.

For the next few minutes the pair walked in near silence, apart from the Apprentice correcting directions and The Messenger trying to avoid igniting the tunnels. Soon the faint echo of their footsteps began to grow louder and the tunnel widened, continuing to grow until it became a large cavern. The cavern was brightly illuminated in various areas by large formations of Glintstone and had a sizable pool of bright blue water at one far side. Next to it was a arrangement of old, abandoned shacks and charred stone houses, remnants of the Indran miners efforts. Barely pausing to appreciate the history the two moved on through the seemingly endless cavern.

"We're close now," the Apprentice finally said, "not long until the plains."

"So what are they?" The Messenger asked, ignoring the statement, "those beasts assaulting Tychus? They're like nothing I've ever seen, monstrous husks of metal and fire. Our own creation, he said, a creation no one knows of."

The Apprentice looked at him sideways in the dull, dusty light, reluctant to speak of the Scourge.

"I want to know," The Messenger said calmly, seeing the reservations in the Apprentices' eyes, "I have to know," he emphasised, "it is my city, after all."

"A creation of man," the Apprentice stated simply, "not mage, not demon but man," he paused for a moment to consider again if a member of such a simple caste could understand but decided either way it was his right to know. "Do you know of The Incursion? It's a good few hundred years back, now?"

"Something about an otherworldly force trying to invade us?" he waved a hand around uninterestedly, trying to grasp the point of its mention.

"Yes, you see, the incursion was only barely defeated by our ancestors-"

"Our?" The Messenger interjected curiously.

"Their defeat was an effort of both man and mage. Yet, this evil was foretold to return with dire consequences to our world. At that point it was decided that a better way to protect ourselves was needed. An army of cataclysmic machines was built, infused with a dark power left behind after The Incursion." At last the cavern began to narrow again and a tunnel became apparent in the far wall, a pinpoint of natural light heralding an exit. "My people didn't agree with the creation of such things, insisting a power such as that could not be tamed. Unsurprisingly we were right, so when you lost control and came crawling to us we constructed a way to stop them. We built the Heart for no other reason than to ensure there were enough of you left to learn a lesson from all this destruction," the

Apprentice stopped walking, realising that, in his anger, he had stormed away, leaving The Messenger several paces behind.

"I knew of none of this," The Messenger spoke softly, not insulted by the Apprentices attitude but rather agreeing with his opinion on the brashness and stupidity of the collected governments, "I simply wish to save my home."

The Apprentice looked to the spark of light in the deep, black tunnel and sighed. "Save it, you will," the Apprentice added at last before striding off along the tunnel without another thought on the subject.

The Messenger lost sight of the Apprentice for some seconds with the contrast of the ever brightening dawn sun against the tunnels blackness hurting his eyes. Eventually he stumbled out into air that seemed burning after the coolness of the caverns. The light flooded his eyes, making nothing but a vague outline of the horizon and the bright sun sitting on it. As he squinted and blinked at the morning, the glare started to fade and he could see that he was at the top of a rocky escarpment against a sheer cliff. The Apprentice was already some way down the scarp, looking over a large, flat desert with the hazy outline of Indra far off in the distance.

"We'll never make it," The Messenger half called to the Apprentice, his heart sinking at the thought of his city in ruins.

"What do you think we are?" the Apprentice asked quietly as The Messenger moved down the slope towards him, "Mystics? Soothsayers? Hermits with no real power?"

"I never question what I don't understand," The Messenger said simply, stepping in line with his counterpart who turned to him and smiled.

"Good answer," he grabbed The Messengers arm harshly and darted forward in a plume of dust, somehow propelling himself across the desert at tremendous speed. As The Messenger was dragged along on the ride of a lifetime, Indra became much clearer, racing towards him as though some great force was pressing it across the land. It became apparent that it was not so much of an abandoned fort but rather an impenetrable fortress, a high tower driving into the sky from its centre.

Soon enough Indras approach slowed to a stop, leaving the pair at the base of a large portcullis surrounded by vast ramparts. In a second the huge gate began to rise with no other command than the Apprentices mere presence. He turned to The Messenger and smiled as several other mages emerged from the innards of the dusty fort.

"The people of this world may think of us what they like but know only that we are far from powerless," the Apprentice turned towards his fellow mages and stepped through the huge opening.

The Messenger hung motionless in the growing heat of the desert morning, trying to overcome the effects of his supersonic dash. He slowly looked up at the central tower piercing the sky above him and breathed out gently. "That's...erm," he tried to muster a suitable, if not accurate, description, "...big," he eventually murmured to himself as the gate creaked and began to fall, forcing him to hurry after the Apprentice.

The inside of the fort was as you would generally expect from an abandoned military position. There were unimpressive stone huts and disused forges around the parade ground, a few mages meandering around as though nothing overly important was happening. In contrast the tower was a shining obsidian black, veins of glowing blue mineral running through the glassy substance like a life force. It was clearly apparent that this was the true majesty of this place, something far beyond the rest of the world. The Messenger gazed at the powerful spire as a strange, unseen energy seemed to want to draw him towards it. A strange, beautiful force that he knew for a fact was dangerous, a force that was currently destroying Tychus. Despite all of his wonder and haunted fears, though, only one thing really occurred to him. "If you people are so powerful then how were you caught by that thing in the forest?"

The words forced the Apprentice and his colleagues to a dead stop at the base of the tower. He thought for a few seconds as the other two turned to face him expectantly. "Just because we are 'so powerful' doesn't mean we can't be taken by surprise," he stated simply at last as the mages around him nodded in content agreement. "Look," he continued, refusing to dwell on the frankly embarrassing instance, "the Heart is ready in the Jump Room."

"Jump Room?" The Messenger asked suspiciously.

The Apprentice looked up. "The top. It's the only place where we can get a good focus."

"The top," The Messenger repeated uncomfortably. "How exactly do we get to 'the top?'" he asked again, once more stepping in line with the Apprentice, "or am I better off not knowing?"

The Apprentice looked sideways at The Messenger. "You're probably better off not knowing." Again the Apprentice roughly grabbed hold of The Messengers arm and rocketed up into the air, allowing the ground to fall away as if it had never meant to be there in the first place. As they sped through the air the obsidian tower became almost translucent and it was possible to see thousands more mages inside. Each of them conducted a variety of wild and amazing experiments utilising a form of the glowing mineral that grew like veins through the tower. Soon enough they began to slow and the Apprentice casually stepped forward into the faded black wall, pulling The Messenger with him, into the tower. Inside was even more amazing than the outside. The entire wall that was expected to encircle them with black rock was completely transparent, allowing for an unnerving yet fantastic view for hundreds of miles all around. In the distance sat a plume of black smoke and flickering lights. This was Tyn Tychus, or at least, what was about to become the remnants of Tyn Tychus. Along the ground pulsed yet more veins of the mineral into a central podium, similar to the one that resided in the city's citadel. Atop it sat a large, elongate object, glowing a brilliantly bright gold.

"This is what you've come for," the Apprentice said simply, "all you have to do is take it, then you can be home," he smiled brightly as The Messenger turned around in confusion. "Why do you think we call it the 'Jump Room?' It can take you anywhere. Absolutely anywhere in this world. In a second it can fly you and the Heart to save Tychus."

The Messenger darted forward aggressively. "If it was that simple then why not do it straight away!?" he shouted, furious that these mages had let his city burn for apparently no reason. "Why didn't you stop them when it all started? Before they attacked Cealathon, before they attacked anywhere?"

The Apprentice sighed and tried to place a calming hand on The Messengers shoulder, only to be swatted away. "It's never just a case of doing it, nothing ever as simple as an action. The Heart would never allow it. It needed a feeling, the feeling that it was truly needed, for a part of what needed saving to reach out and touch it. That, my friend, is exactly what you have done," he tried to place his hand on The Messengers shoulder again, only this time it was allowed as he stared out towards his home, far across the silent land.

The Messenger opened his mouth to speak but, instead, just shook his head and took a step towards the pedestal.

"Just think of home," the Apprentice spoke softly while The Messenger climbed the shallow steps to the Heart, the veins pulsing under his feet.

"Home," The Messenger repeated, reaching out to lay a finger on the Heart. It was chillingly cold but had a soothing quality to it, humming at he wrapped his hand around it.

"I never did ask," the Apprentice stated, making The Messenger turn around only to see him at the end of a twisting tunnel made up mostly of colours he could never have imagined existed, "what's your name?"

"My name?" The Messenger murmured as the tunnel grew ever longer, disorientating all of his senses. Finally he managed to look at the fading image of the Apprentice and gather his words. "My name is Isolar and I am a Messenger." Just as he spoke the tunnel pulsed and threw back on its self, knotting existence into never to be considered permutations and thwarting its own understanding of its self. The tunnel strobed and fell, briefly allowing The Messenger to catch glimpses of ill considered realities and far away places. Suddenly it swung back, jarring The Messenger back into logical knowing and forced him through a wall of the brightest white, beyond which was Tychus and the monstrous army besieging it.

From atop the citadel The Messenger looked out at a sight he could barely believe, his jaw slowly falling open. With the dawning of the sun, the black mist had cleared leaving only the ranks of metal legs crashing down over the crumbling city walls. Their huge bulks heaved over the burning remains of the market district below. Above him the cannons still roared, defiant in the face of defeat, their ammunition ricocheting from the thick shells of the Scourge, only occasionally stumbling them. Then from nowhere a huge metal claw swiped overhead, knocking The Messenger to the ground and decapitating the citadel, destroying the cities last means of defence. He tried to stagger to his feet again as rubble crashed down all around with thick dust consuming him. Suddenly he was halted by a huge figure looming towards him, two rows of four eyes each glowing a deep red against the veil of dust. Slowly it moved closer, the creatures huge iron mandibles piercing through the settling dust as it stamped a spike ended leg into the ground next to The Messenger. He managed to get to his feet, glancing around for a way to escape, the abomination still baring down on him. Just as it was about to strike, The Messenger spotted an open hatch amongst the pummelled stone blocks and immediately darted towards it, leaping through as the war machine demolished yet more of the citadels upper towers.

With no time to recover from the fall, The Messenger scrambled to his feet again and tried to run from a metallic leg piercing the ceiling, driving down into the body of the fortress. He clutched the Heart tightly to his chest as the leg was pulled back, effortlessly tearing a gaping void through the side of the building. He kept running through the wide halls of the citadel towards the Inner Sanctum, not looking back in case the ground gave way beneath him. Occasionally, through the arrow slits in the heavy walls, he caught glances of the machines outside, reducing the city beneath them to pulverised rubble. These did not concern him, though. Rather he feared the one lurking just beyond the wall, capable of ending his life and the hopes of the city in a second. Instead it waited, choosing, he thought, to toy with its victim to the last second, where it could cause the greatest desperation and loss.

Soon enough The Messenger made it to the sanctum and moved straight towards the pedestal, somehow guided as though the Heart were whispering to him. As if in a trance he bolted past The Regent, who was huddled into a corner holding something tight to her, and pulled The Heart from his tunic. In one fluid motion he placed it firmly into a perfectly shaded slot in the pedestal and stepped back expectantly.

Nothing happened.

"The Heart?" groaned The Regent, looking up towards The Messenger and the glowing artefact as it continued to stand, seemingly inert, "the Mages Apprentice?"

"Is a liar!" The Messenger snapped, swinging around, "he sent me back with nothing! A useless ornament!"

"The Heart is only part of it," she moved her hand, revealing her dress to be soaked with blood and a shard of metal protruding from her chest, "it needs to know them, feel their dark energy so that it may cleanse it," she sharply wrenched the fragment from herself and offered it up with a shaking hand. "I waited," she wavered, making The Messenger start running towards her, "I fear I have waited too long," she ended at last, her body going limp, allowing the shard to tumble through the air for a moment. As it clattered to the ground the entire back wall was demolished inward, forcing The Messenger to the ground again. Through the settling dust that beast stood again, its front two legs perched on the wall, almost smug, if it knew of such a thing, at its ability to torment. The Messenger coughed and pushed himself up, rubble falling from his back. He gazed at the body of the city's leader, then down at the thing she had given her life for. Again, something told him what to do, like he had always been meant to.

Quickly he scooped up the bloodied fragment of metal and dove towards the pedestal again with the machine striking a claw forward to stop him. Just before the huge metal arm struck him, The Messenger pierced The Hearts crystalline surface with the shard and a cloud of black static moved between them. Immediately a bubble of the brightest light pulsed out from the pedestal with a deafening screech, making the Heart shatter. It radiated out across the city, beyond the walls, through Gallowtrees and Glintstone and far further than anyone could ever know. In that moment of immense power the metal beasts, which had just about reached the Residential District, froze solid. The red glow in their eyes faded to an obtuse black and every last one began collapsing.

When the shrill tone had eventually faded The Messenger opened his eyes slowly and found his nemesis slumped against what was left of the Citadels wall.

"Who are you!?" a voice shouted from behind.

"No one," The Messenger responded automatically, as he would have with anyone on the streets, "just a Messenger," he added, turning around to see The Captain in the torn and dirty remnants of his armour.

"You retrieved The Heart?" The Captain asked, looking about at the clear slithers of glass on the ground.

"I just brought it back," The Messenger started, "the Mages Apprentice showed me the way, I didn't really do-"

"You did everything, boy! I don't know how you found out about it but the important thing is that you took the initiative. You're a hero, son," he smiled at The Messenger for a second before spotting The Regent, half buried in debris, "one of a few on this day," he crouched down and started to brush the dust from her. "She knew what was needed and was determined to retrieve it in any way possible. I tried to stop her, go in her place but she just walked off towards them, alone," he hung his head for a second and then looked up again. "Yes, though, a hero! You should be treated as one!" he harshly grabbed The Messengers arm and pulled him towards the open wall, stepping out onto the corpse of the metal beast, without fear, as a huge crowd started to gather below. "Today!" he shouted across the remains of the city, "we have lost so much. Yet still, on this day, we emerge victorious!" His words prompted a huge cheer from the crowd. "For this we have two to thank. Our wise Regent who, I am sad to say, gave her life so that ours may go on and this simple Messenger," he rose The Messengers arm high into the air. "I can't even begin to imagine what he went through to bring back our salvation. With the Regent gone it is my duty to take rule over this city for the time being. However, as this city lays in ruins I declare that we must start anew!" Another roar of applause went up from the crowd, forcing The Captain to wait some time until it died down. "I feel it is only fair that we honour this hero among men, this Messenger who has saved us all. In light of our situation, our new home will be named after this simple saviour," he turned to The Messenger and grinned, "what is your name, Messenger?"

"Um," he started, overwhelmed by the honour that was being bestowed upon him, "Isolar," he ended shakily.

"Then from now on Tyn Tychus is no more! From the rubble that has been left today will rise Tyn Isolar!" One final, enormous roar went up from the crowd, this time spreading across what was left of the city until every survivor was chanting Isolars name.

Over time The Messengers and those like them, died out. Their services were transcended by ever faster, more efficient methods of delivery. If not for that one Messenger the entire caste would have faded away, their entire existence completely forgotten. Yet, for hundreds of years to come tales were still told, not only of the great Isolar but of every Messenger. They were no longer undesirables among society, avoided at all costs but an icon of trust. An example of what good could come from every person, no matter who they were, if they had the desire to do so. Even now Tyn Isolar still stands, a shining beacon for the entire land. The City of Peace.

End of World

With the winter drawing in and the nights lengthening it almost seemed as though the sun would never return. Yet every morning, even if it were late, the sun would rise over the world, bringing warmth and comfort back to the hearts of everyone under it. What if it didn't, though? What if the sun set and never came up again? What if night lived on continuously, allowing the creatures that lurk in the shadows to do their bidding across the world? The Earth and everything in it would fall like a rock, just because the sun didn't come up anymore. Your life would be dominated by avoiding the despicable creatures and the only light would be from the flames licking across the horizon...That's when you wake up in a cold sweat, praying that the creatures haven't got into your house while you unwittingly slipped into a eerily calm sleep. As you gaze around the dark room, into the shadows, a chill strikes up your spine and catches you unaware, making you look up and out of the window at the dark sky. Slowly you begin to think about the absence of that haunting glow from the fires off in the distance. With courage you manage to get up and walk to the window. Outside everything is calm, the night is dark but the street lamp on the corner casts a reassuring pool of light on the pavement. You begin to contemplate that it was all a nightmare but you still can't help thinking what if... What if it wasn't a dream? What if the sun wasn't going to rise again? You eventually go back to your bed and once again try to peacefully sleep, all the time with that nagging thought at the back of your mind, what if…

The sun finally began to spill over the horizon and I breathed a sigh of relief. Even so the thought of that dream was still with me. I couldn't shake the feeling that it was more than just any normal dream. I wondered whether I was loosing my mind, but soon abandoned the thought for the aspiration of breakfast. As I walked to the kitchen, no matter how I tried, I still couldn't get it out of my head. Every time I closed my eyes, there it was again, the horizon on fire, with those creatures everywhere. I composed myself and looked through the window. The only thing wrong with the horizon today was the city's smog obscuring the skyline, yet that wasn't exactly out of the ordinary. I sat at my table and switched the news on, only to be greeted with the general terrors you had come to expect from the modern world. Once again troops had died in Iraq, there was an oil spillage in the North Sea and none of the governments really knew what to do with themselves. I was just beginning to relax and forget about my dream when they said it. "A meteorite hit the North Midlands last night…" I saw it in my head, the pitted countryside that used to be England, now charred with flames licking at what vegetation there was left. The television buzzed and brought me round again. "…The meteor was thought to have been approximately the size of a football and is reportedly a fragment from a much larger body currently passing close to Earth. The public is asked not to panic as scientists advise that the meteor is passing well outside of Earth's orbit." Even with these words a chill still shot up my spine.

They began talking about statistics which really didn't interest me so I turned to see to breakfast. I was alerted back to the television only when it began crackling with increasing intensity. Static spread across the screen and panic slowly spread across the reporters face. Suddenly the camera was thrown round and it seemed like they were running, jerked images showed a huge fireball steaking through the early morning mist. The camera was abruptly dropped and seconds later there was an immense explosion, then the picture was gone, yet I could still hear the explosion. I hurried to the door just in time to see the mushroom cloud rise and spread out over the land…but how…the Midlands was over 230 miles away. And then none of it mattered anymore because it was coming. I could feel the wind start to blow, the heat intensify. I ran in search for cover but I was too late. The shockwave hit and I was thrown across the street along with my house with the heat boiling my skin. The last thing I remember was thinking that I was dead already and then being swept away by the scorching dust cloud.

The lad couldn't have been much older than seventeen. He looked out of a crack in the rubble up on to the street above. The blast had obviously destroyed everything worth speaking of and I assumed that we were now in the remnants of someone's cellar. The rest of the house was collapsed above us, sealing us down here, beyond that I had no idea. As if with surprise I realized that I was awake and with a certain amount of shame I became aware that I'd been awake for several minutes now. Questions began to flood into my mind, various ones about what had happened but most of all about that lad, still looking cautiously through the crack. He had terrible burns to his arms but only minor injuries on his face. He had obviously shielded his face from the heat wave with his arms when it had hit. He had other wounds, though, different from the burns and gashes you'd expect. Along the side of his chest and again on his face I saw, now, that there were slices, almost as though he'd been slashed with a knife several times. His injuries made me think of my own predicament. I scuffled to sit up properly, unaware that I could have lost any or all my major appendages. With the sound of my futile attempts to gain purchase the lad turned around sharply and I stopped. He breathed out and fell against the wall.

"Thank God, I though you were dead," he said trying to regain his breath. He was obviously scared of something and by the looks of what he'd been through, I didn't blame him. "This place is safe from what's out there…" he nodded towards the crack leading outside, "but it could collapse at any time, so we really need to get out as soon as we can."

I couldn't help thinking what kind of dangers were now 'out there' but my mind was brought back to the more immediate point. "Get out of here? I don't even know where 'here' is."

"It's a building on Wards Street, or at least what used to be Wards Street," he looked at the charred walls, seemingly in remorse, "it came down when I was searching it. I managed to get down here before the walls collapsed. The floor above seems to be holding for now but I don't know how long it will be that way."

I couldn't believe it, this was my house, although it'd obviously ceased to look like my house a long while ago. I again tried to get up and again failed.

"I wouldn't do that," the lad gestured to a rudimentary splint on my leg, "I suppose St. Johns Ambulance wasn't such a bad idea, in the end."

"I should think 'what happened?' would be the most obvious question," I mused, pointing to his side and knowing full well that the answer wasn't going to be pretty.

"After the meteor hit a whole lot of people died, you couldn't move for the bodies. A group of survivors banded together to support each other, that's who I got separated from," his eyes told me more then he was letting on, that group had been through a lot and I suspected that they'd become like family to each other. "Then, one day, the bodies were gone, just gone, no trace. There are rumours, but I can assure you, though, that they're not rumours. There are creatures out there…"

Those words triggered something in my mind and I remembered that dream on the night before the meteor struck.

"They take the bodies," he said weakly, "of both the living and the dead." The dream flashed through my mind again and I saw them, twisted and deformed with the blood of their victims on their-

"You were attacked weren't you?" I spoke sudden and fast, driven by the rapidly diminishing chance that it was a dream.

The lad nodded. "It jumped me when I was scavenging. It clawed me and tried to get me with this weird tube thing. I think that's what they do, suck your blood or something. I was lucky, though, it heard someone coming and fled. They're easily enough spooked but I doubt their gonna be shy for much longer. You see there have been more attacks lately and people are going missing."

Something outside startled the lad and he ducked down, peering awkwardly through the gap in the rubble. I could hear footsteps outside and dust was kicked through the gap in the rubble onto the lad but he didn't even flinch.

"Jase? Jason, man, are you here?" came a lowered voice from beyond the wall of debris. I was surprised to hear another voice, some part of me still didn't believe that people had actually survived.

"Guy?" whispered the lad getting up, "is that you?"

"Jason! Where are you?" I could see the soles of Guy's shoes suddenly start moving around in a frenzy.

"Down here," he reached through the gap and waved up some dust, "I've found someone, get help."

The feet went running off and I remember seeing the lad, who I now knew to be called Jason, slump down, grinning and then nothing much else. I knew we were rescued, but after that everything was a blur. We were taken back to some kind of bomb shelter but after that we just survived. No purpose to our lives. Just existing on rations and condensation, barely managing to keep each other sane. Then around three weeks later something happened.

By this time, I'd heard about the fires raging all around. Since the meteor had struck the temperature had gone up, supposedly it was the same all over the planet and, if the rumours were anything to go by, soon strong acid would begin to fall in the rain. Eventually the fires would run out of things to burn and die down, leaving the whole world cloaked in a veil of smoke and ash. It wasn't like you'd be able to see the sun now, let alone after the fires had been raging for weeks on end. But there would come a time when all the fires would cease and the temperature would plummet. Something akin to a nuclear winter I would suspect, a seemingly endless, desperately cold night were vicious electrical storms would constantly rage overhead. Some future to look forward to, we'd be lucky to survive a week longer in here, let alone out there. If that wasn't enough, Jason had been right. The creatures were becoming more confident and now they were readily roaming the streets. We had already lost three more people on scavenging runs, as if there was much left to scavenge.

The acid rain had begun to fall in the last few days confining us in the shelter. Just as well, I suppose, over the last few nights there had been strange noises outside. Scratching on the side of the shelter. Shallow, sounds that were eerily hushed and soothing. Some said it was the wind in the trees, but I knew it wasn't, there weren't any trees out there anymore. I dreaded every night, fearing I would not wake up, but tonight was something else.

After a few hours of sleeplessness the scratching, the curious sounds all suddenly stopped. In any other situation this would have been a good thing but these creatures were persistent, they wouldn't have given up just like that. Against all better judgment one of my new associates took curiosity and ultimately faith to heart and proceeded towards the hatch. He was convinced it was a sign, a signal to us that the rain had stopped, the creatures gone and the world was ready for us again. Against all our better judgements he quickly open the hatch, swinging it out into the world. There, for the first time in days I caught a glimpse of the outside. It wasn't what I remembered. The winter had firmly set in, the acid rain destroying everything familiar to me. The sky was now sprawled with thick black clouds laced with an odd green tinge. Through them blue and purple lightning struck silently. I looked down at the ground and saw nothing. The ground was charred lifeless and there were skeletons of trees as far as the eye could see. As for the city, well, there was no longer any city. Just the husk of past achievements.

The acid rain had, indeed, finally stopped and my brave colleague cautiously took his first steps into the changed world. What was left of his shoes hissed as they touched the ground. He took a few steps and then with more confidence began to walk out into, what could only be described as, the desert of civilization. Soon he left our view but no one could bring themselves to look out for him.

"Where'd he go?" a woman at the back of the shelter mouthed quietly.

Suddenly there was a rapturous clang on the front end of our steel shelter, making everyone jerk back. We looked, terrified at the ajar hatch, then slowly something began to slide from the roof into the doorway. Our foolhardy companion was dead. His head had been ripped half off and his torso was sliced open allowing his insides to trial behind the main bulk of his body from the roof. No one had the breath to scream, we all just stared at the doorway, trapped in a terror induced trance. I don't know how long passed, but waiting seemed like a lifetime. Ironic really that we felt like we had to wait a lifetime in order to die. Then slowly and silently three long, grey fingers reached around and with a deliberate flowing motion gripping the frame of the hatch. The creatures head began to emerge from around the frame. It was as grey as its fingers and had three huge bug like eyes, each with a strange red tint to them. It had no apparent mouth, only a long tube that curled up and down, swaying with the creatures gentle movements. Even though it had no mouth in order to do so, something in its eerily proportioned eyes told me it was grinning. I watched as it hung in the doorway motionless, every bit of my essence saying that I wasn't going to survive this. I could feel the terror of everyone else in the shelter pressing against the back of my neck, forcing the hairs up. Normally I would have shivered, but instead it made me realize that, even if I wanted to, I couldn't move. I was frozen, some primordial command telling my body to become as stone. Every tendon in my body was so tight that I was convinced every single one would instantly snap if I moved. Then for some reason I began to relax. The creature was still there but now somehow I wasn't as afraid of it. I could feel something from it, then as if it had never been there in the first place, it turned, its glistening skin reflecting what little light there was, and left.

I looked around to see that everyone was still ridged with fear so cautiously approached the hatch. There was nothing out there, no life, no sky, not even fires on the horizon, which had become the norm of late, there was only the bitterly cold air biting at my face. Most importantly the creatures were gone, I didn't know where and I didn't really care. I looked back into the shelter, thinking more about what the rest of our lives were going to be like, then the more immediate situation of why the creatures had just given up their attack. Just as I was about to re-enter the shelter a whooshing sound emanated from far behind me. I turned again and in the distance I saw what seemed to be a flare shoot up from the remnants of Greater London. The flare began to fall back to the ground. As soon as it did there were a number of additional whooshing sounds and a dozen or so more flares flew up into the air. That's when I knew, these weren't flares, they were rudimentary rockets of some kind. There were survivors there and they were retaliating. It would explain why the creatures left in such a hurry. I tried to inform the others about the happenings but they had already figured it out for themselves. There was now a buzz of people stating their desire to help and how they would prefer to go out fighting. So that was it, with the last strength we had in us we began to head back to London, with one hope and one hope alone…survival.

By the time we reached the outer city limits it must have been getting on for dawn. It was hard to tell with the global ash cloud sprawled across the sky, blotting out the sun. None the less, it seemed as though the fighting had ceased and I had a disturbing feeling that the retaliation had not prevailed. Soon we managed to find the site of the battle. There were large lines of piled rubble with substantial breaches in them and a number of rudimentary weapons strewn around the site. This had obviously been where the barricades had fallen. Bodies were scattered about amongst the rubble, Most were human but it looked as though they had managed to take a fair few of the creatures with them before they were overwhelmed.

Looking about at the death and destruction around me a powerful feeling came over me. I thought back to that question 'what would life be like, now?' What were everyone's lives going to be like? Just then I heard them, they were calling to me, they were calling to everyone. They had always been calling but now it was noticeable. With the silence of our own species we could hear them. Again we started walking, towards and through the devastated barricade, just this time something was pulling us. In the distance I could hear the distraught cries of mothers for their children, the moans of despair. These were nothing but the sounds of people still with hope and hope was something I was rapidly beginning to give up on.

The exodus of our people continued in the distance yet, to me at least, it all seemed like a blur. I walked onwards through the jungle of wreckage and out into the charred countryside. Before I knew what had happened I was standing on a hillside overlooking a vast plain. There was silence. The calling had ceased and I couldn't even hear the low, icy breeze as it passed across the low lying common. Something then scratched at my ears, some low tone that passed through me and should have made me shudder, yet it did not. It resonated around me, gaining strength and pitch. Its beat was like that of a heart, but its eerie intensity seemed to slow, the momentum of the beat failed and as quickly as it had become known to me, it was almost gone, then with one last, defiant beat, it ceased.

The breeze returned to me and I looked upon the true sight of what was below. Hundreds upon thousands of bodies littered the blood soaked ground, only they were not human. Then I realized, it had never been us who were being hunted. These creatures were a bigger part of this world than we could have ever imagined, but we had been exploiting and abusing both them and this world alike for far too long now. That is why they had come. They were the essence of nature and they had brought the meteor in an attempt to put an end to humanities kamikaze existence. Man had brought war, though, the trait he had become most skilled in. Weapons, technology and the will to dominate were brought forth, slaughtering these cleansers, leaving the fate of the world firmly in the hands of those who could not be trusted with it in the first place.

With the breeze came the mournful song of Dolphins in an ocean across the horizon, they sung for salvation and also to mourn for the End of World.

I don't know what happened. We had just found out about the special services being flown in from Sydney and of our victory over the aliens on the common, when we found he was gone. After finding the barricades he just started walking. We all thought that he knew something we didn't but after getting caught up with the refugees, we lost him. As soon as we knew where our victory had occurred, more then just a few of us wanted to see if the news was true. We hurried to the cliff overlooking the common to get the best view, just I guess no one saw what they expected to. We arrived there just in time to see him fall. I don't know what had possessed him to jump. I had been stuck in that hovel with him for a long time now so I figured I knew him well enough. I never would have thought he would do anything like this. It must have been the whole idea of what the rest of his life was going to be like. I suppose it was the thought of having no home to go back to, hardly even any world left at all. I've seen things, now, things no person should see. I have no doubt they could drive people to acts you would never have thought possible. In the end they can save us but more often than not we are beyond salvation.

Soul

Looking up at Neptune, leering so greatly in the sky, it's hard to fathom how far we are from home. I barely believed how dim and cold the sun could shine here but a world where it doesn't shine at all? From my window I watched the strange plants sway majestically in the undetectable breeze and my mind was cast back to home. To her. Before it happened we always used to lie on the grass in my garden and watch the clouds skim across the deep blue sky. There is no sky here, only the purple haze that drifts in front of the stars, constantly reminding me that I am so far away and she is gone.

There was a knock at my door and the site representative edged in. "How are you settling?" I nodded quickly without turning to him. "I'm aware she didn't make it," he continued, "I'm sorry for your loss."

"'It happens,' they told me," I looked down at the white rose in my hand. She had given it to me just before we left for the transport. It had wilted and began to brown but it was the only thing I had left of Earth. The only thing linking me to a lost life. "These things don't just 'happen.' I only lost sight of her for a minute. It was long enough to be consumed by the crowd, though."

The representative hung his head. He had heard any number of stories just the same since landing but none were any easier to hear. "Orientation is in twenty minutes," he said at last, hovering in the hatchway of my small bunkroom for a few seconds more in silence. "Feel free to look around the complex and the surrounding area, god knows this place needs exploring. Just don't wander too far," he waited for a while longer, watching me cradle the dying rose before silently leaving.

I continued to stare out at the alien landscape and watched as another lifeboat ship touched down in the blast pit. Every time another landed I felt a spark of hope telling me that she had somehow made it, but every time I knew it was false hope. I had seen it before, no one ever got out of those crowds let alone onto another ship. After a lifeboat left it all turned to hell. No one cared about anything anymore, they just tore each other apart, civilisation collapsed and in the end there was nothing left.

The refugees poured from the ship, haggard and filthy, not yet even caring where they had landed, just elated to be free from the cramped capsule. I should know, everyone here should have know what it was like. Those twelve days spent barely able to move, no food, hardly any water. It felt like an eternity. I turned away from the Plexiglas window, not wanting to remember anymore, and slowly started down one of the claustrophobic tunnels towards orientation.

Every single person in the auditorium looked the same. They looked exactly how I felt. Every one of them had lost it all; lives, loved ones, everything they had ever known. The seminar its self was only what could have been expected given how many bureaucrats had been brought. System of government, distribution of work and provisions, all too much about 'our bright future'. Soon it was over, though, and I was on my way back to my cramped bunk. Despite the supposedly inspiring words by our leaders, nobody said even a word to one another on the way out. They didn't understand how we felt. How could they? They hadn't lost anything. Their families and their status, everything had come with them. For all it meant, none of it mattered. I just stared out of that window once again, watching as they dismantled the tin cans they called space ships for recycling. This really was a unusual place. Strange mists drifted all around, suspended in the middle air, shapes glided high above and the plants that surrounded the settlement. No matter how

I felt their gentle sway somehow settled my mind, soft colours from the Neptunian sky glinting off their slick, fleshy skin. In the crisis of it all no one had considered the possibility of life out here. Even now, when we were faced with this lurid alien ecosystem it did little to stir that curious nature in most of us. It was just yet another thing we had to take in our stride. This as with everything else; the loss of loved ones, the passing of all we knew, the destruction of our very world, it just had to be dealt with.

Even so, the place worked to ease my warring emotions, extruding a placid embrace that had already settled my feelings somewhat since our arrival. I considered if that was the reason they had chosen this place. Maybe there was some naturally occurring sedative in the air here. Undoubtedly a small, calm and docile populous was easier to control than the raging urban sprawls that had developed on Earth. It mattered little to me how they would try to control this bastion of humanity. Sooner of later everyone would realise that we would have to work together if we had any hope of surviving. Even those who considered themselves so high and mighty, the leaders among men, would have to join in with the rest of us in the toil of building our future. In that thought I was reminded of what the representative had mentioned of exploration. In the bleakness of my salvation, the survivors guilt and, despite how anyone else felt, nothing excited me more than exploring a whole new world. After all, it was the most literal sense of escapism, the dream of turning your back on the turmoil of your past life to find an entirely new reality.

Finally placing the wilted, drying rose head on the rim of the viewport I made my way down to one of the supplementary airlocks, with the primary ones still too crammed with clamouring refugees to be of any use. Although the atmosphere on this world was breathable, filtered air was still pumped into the complex and you had to go through decontamination every time you wanted to enter or leave. The logical reason would be to think there was some concern around particles or alien bacteria. As with the majority of things, though, it was much more bureaucratic. It had probably been designed like it was because that's how people expected it to be. To have an off world complex which *didn't* have complex airlocks and filtration units simply didn't seem right and tended to make people suspicious. Apparently yet another ploy to subdue the general population, meet expectations and keep everyone quiet.

There was only one attendant stood on duty to open the way to the shimmering haze outside. Upon noticing my approach, without a word, she turned and retrieved a belt with a facemask and small canister marked 'O2' hooked onto it. As soon as I took it she quickly turned and pressed a large button to one side of two large doors which slid apart with a short hiss. Turning back she stood, expectantly staring at me whilst I fumbled to clip the belt around my waist. It was clear that this was just another attempt at meeting peoples expectations. If it wasn't then there would have been a briefing on how to use the mask properly, some instructions or at least a concern about the fact I was having difficulty equipping it. Instead there was just an uncomfortable impatience radiating from the attendant, clearly assigned this task for the simple reason that someone had to do it and it didn't really matter who. Eventually I managed to clip the awkward buckle together and the small gas tank fell loosely to my side, hanging surprisingly heavily against my leg. Again, there was that expectant look as she waited for me to step into the unnecessary airlock, so I quickly complied. No sooner as I had moved past the small rooms magnetic seal did the doors hiss shut behind me. I felt a mild pressure growing in the front of my head as the atmosphere was filtered out, replaced with that of the outside. Soon enough the pair of exterior doors gasped and parted with a muffled hiss where my ears had not yet equalised to the pressure. It was something to look out at this place but to be out here was something completely different. A fine, violet mist lapped at my feet and I choked for a second, reconsidering my initial stance on the face masks. During the meeting there had been something about the composition of the air here having a higher concentration of Argon. All anyone heard, though, was 'not dangerous.' Even so I hadn't expected it to catch my breath like it did.

I took a deep gulp of air and started off into the alien wilderness. There were no fences, no real edge to the compound and you had to use your own judgement when knowing how far to venture out. I was afraid to admit to myself that my own judgement was sorely lacking as I wandered far into the bizarre landscape. It felt like something was at my back, pressing me further out, away from any form of civilisation. Without looking back I knew that the compound was quickly falling away over the horizon and would be near impossible to find again lest I turned back now. I was only kidding myself, though, as the compound had already long since been obscured by the strange mist, its form distorted and broken by the shimmering air. I stopped for a second and thought about what I was doing. It wasn't so much as a revelation to my mind as more of a new awareness. I was lost. Far away from any form of home in a world I neither knew or cared for. Despite my anticipation of it, the swell of panic at being alone out here, the fear of never getting back, it never rose from the pit of my stomach. Then I realised why. I was already about as far away from home as I could be anyway. I was already alone, no chance of ever going back. All the fear and panic I would experience had already been and gone, thrust on me when I caught a last glance of the dwindling Earth from the lifeboat. It had raced away so quickly, become so small so soon.

I slumped down on a large boulder and inspected a small bioluminescent plant as it swayed gently in all directions, apparently ignoring the fundamental force that was gravity. At least out here it was quiet. I was unsure if I should or not but out here I had the option to think. Think about all that had happened to me, to the whole of humanity. Instead my mind was drawn to thoughts of colonisation, frontier folk travelling out here to start a new, away from the old governments that had the misfortune of surviving. Soon there would be towns everywhere, maybe even colonies on some of the other moons that were faintly visible against Neptune's bright glow. Soon the concept 'lost' would be as it had become on Earth; all but extinct.

I withdrew from the strange plant, feeling guilty that it, along with all forms of unique and amazing life on this world would eventually fall to the humans who trampled with such voraciousness. Would this place fall victim to the plague of Man as our own planet had? It wasn't a thought I savoured. There was no justification for us to take other worlds as though we were divinely entitled, no excuse for us to do what we pleased with them.

As those sentiments drifted through my mind, so too did a chorus of agreement. They weren't actual words, just feelings, reinforcement of the precedent I had proposed. Only, the agreements, they were not my own. They couldn't be, there were too many of them. They spoke with me like a thousand voices, each more abrasive than the last but soothed into a unified flow by a single meaning. I felt the voices probe my mind, reaching into every facet of what I was. I didn't know what to do, had no idea what was happening. Even now, I still wasn't scared and I started to consider whether the feeling was even possible for me anymore. It was something different, though, I wasn't scared because I knew there wasn't anything to be scared of. Throughout the whole time they were in my mind there was one overriding message of safety, that they meant no harm. They made it known that, at any time, I could close off a part of myself and they would not attempt to invade. So I just sat on that boulder, bewildered as an unseen force rummaged through my thoughts like I would have searched a cupboard.

Eventually they withdrew, apparently satisfied they had rummaged sufficiently and I was left feeling surprisingly alone. I remained seated, unmoving for quite some time more, waiting for whatever may come next. Nothing did. It had been a whirlwind of the unknown and now, without notice, it had gone. I pushed myself up from the rock and felt a chill in the air. It was time to head back, that is if I could find the way back.

"*Why go?*" asked a single voice, echoed as if carried on the wind. The independence of the voice, its singular nature seemed eerie after all of those exploring thoughts. "*Why return to those who would sadden you?*" The voice didn't so much speak to me than rather imply its meaning through complex feelings and emotions, some of which I had never even dreamt of considering.

I thought about how to respond or whether to respond at all. As the multitude of questions and possible replies flowed through my mind it was like that voice plucked out the most relevant to proceed with.

"Why *do you have to go back?*"

I moved to vocalise my thoughts as instinct dictated but paused short, intrigued by the idea of this higher form of communication.

"*It's home now,*" I thought, feeling it unnecessary to try and project the words in any way. I merely let the essence of what might have otherwise become speech drift through my mind and it was understood. It could never be an awkward, poorly phrased shamble of words. it was always the pure meaning of what you wanted to communicate. "*My people are there...*" I added at last. I wasn't sure why I had put it as I had 'My people.' I didn't even know if this voice in my head was part of a *different* type of people. It could have all caught up on me, for all I knew. I could have been having a psychotic episode. As it transpired, I wasn't. In fact it was the clearest outlook I was given since leaving Earth.

"*I know of them,*" the essence assured calmly, "*they are all as lost as you. We can help.*"

Finally the question I had been trying to avoid slipped to the forefront of my thoughts. The presence questioned its self whether I would be capable of understanding the answer.

"*I am everything here. I am the nothingness you feel when you are alone. I am the air you feel on your face. I am not only of this world, this world is of me. It is of all of us, all of us and the single being we are.*"

The cryptic assault on my comprehension boggled my already confused mind. It was clear the meaning had been greatly simplified for my apparently primitive cortex but in that simplification a great part of its meaning had been lost.

"*Only to be us you would understand our existence.*"

"*You are the soul of this planet?*" I considered tentatively, trying to hold back weak and unimportant musings.

"*I like this name. Soul. Your idea of it is pure and beautiful. Of a sort, I am this world, but this world is also me.*" Its voice fell silent for a moment and my sorrow fell upon me again like a weight. Only I was not reminded of it until it had already returned. It was as though I was feeling my own sadness reflected back by this strange, ethereal being. "*I feel you are still alone. Even though I am with you, I feel you are not with us.*"

Out of the low lying mist a shape began to form. It rose out of the drifting fog, taking the shape of a person as it went. Features began to form, spirit like hair tumbled down its back and I couldn't believe what I was witnessing. "Why her?" I asked out loud, my mind too ablaze with emotion to articulate anything else.

"This is the most comforting form for you." To my surprise the ghostly figure vocalised back in a way I couldn't begin to understand. Its voice reminded me of her. Hearing it in that faint, shallow way made me feel as though she was speaking to me herself, from across the void between here and Earth.

"I'm not sure if I would say comforting," I stood up and took a step towards the misty figure that watched me happily. "What do you want?"

"To help," she replied simply, raising her translucent hand to my face. "Why did you come here? Why did your kind settle on this world?"

It was a valid point. None of us had properly considered why we had landed here, of all places. There had been no word on any significant resources or even bodies of water. It had only been discovered there was life here when the first lifeboats landed. If anything those pioneering Mars colonies would have been a better choice, even in spite of the fact there was no breathable air there. Then it hit me, why the complex had airlocks and oxygen masks at all.

"We felt your pain from across the gulf. Felt you wanted to start a new. We called you, changing our home so that it would be yours. The first of you struggled here but as we grew to know you we could work to sustain you."

"You 'called' us?" I asked, unbelieving of the outrageous tale.

"And you came," she answered again simply. "This is how it has been for an age of the galaxy. All races face the end. They face what they truly are and what they could become. Those who choose to become more are called."

"By you?" I asked forcefully, now really feeling I had lost my mind.

"Or by others. We are not like you but you could be like us. This is the nature of our being. Those who aspire to more are brought to us and, over time, often millennia or more, they become us... *You* become us."

My temper snapped. I felt like I had been lured into some trap to be consumed by a predator. "How could you do this?! You see a dying race so you decide to get your thrills from giving them hope just to use us for your own means?!" I turned to the way I thought I had come from and started walking as fast as I could but her voice was still there in my head. It forced me to a halt as she spoke inside me again.

"You know our purpose is not that. You have felt the truth of what we are, seen what your people will eventually become. Many of your people speak of a place they call 'Heaven.' The reward after you depart this..." her presence took joy from many of the human terms she had found but this one especially so, *"this 'mortal coil.' Your race is dead. We are your heaven."*

I couldn't deny any of it. I *had* seen what we could be. She made sure that was the first thing she had imprinted on my mind. But it seemed all too fast. I was still sad, angry, we all were, nothing was about to change that in a hurry. Even so, I turned around to see her still stood there, drifting loosely in the air. "And are you my angel, then?"

Even though it was just an alien manifestation of the woman I had loved, when it smiled I was still filled with the same, deep, sense that I had felt when she had given me that white rose. The sense that everything was going to be alright.

Humanity had faced a lot in its time. For thousands of years we had killed each other, destroyed the world around us but at the end it hadn't been that which destroyed us. Rather some freak act of nature. Now, though, on the brink of our end there were few enough of us left so that we could see as one. Face the future together and create something wonderful. Just as Soul had for an eternity before, we   were   becoming   something   better.

Plague

S even days, that's all it ever took…

On the first day the eyes swell and their blood vessels begin to release making the afflicted effectively weep blood. The constant layer across the iris gives a red tint to the world. On the second and third days tear ducts begin producing a puss which mixes with the congealing blood to create brown mucus that changes an individual's sight from red to a dark yellow. The third and forth days hold vomiting of thick green bile and the fifth and sixth days result in painful blue bruises around the eyes as the infection spreads back along the optic nerve. Finally on the seventh day: Death.

They call it the Spectrum virus. Supposedly some mutated hybrid of MRSA with a super strain of one foreign flu or another. No-one seemed to have any idea how it had occurred and no-one really cared after the first million died. In the end the reports told us that the plague had spread all around the globe and none of the outside cities were habitable anymore. Those of us who had not been infected were isolated in specially built complexes; so called 'Safe Sectors'. The virus was cunning, though, it could lay dormant in a host for months without so much as a sniffle and then before anyone knew what was happening, everything in the entire sector was dead. It happened at over two thirds of the isolated zones but then it just stopped. With the majority of the human race devastated and our species on the brink of extinction, it just stopped. The people rejoiced as hope returned that the safe sectors that remained were, indeed, safe and the virus had died with the last of the infected.

But it was never about to be that simple. Statistics had always told us that there was at least one last person carrying the virus and as a result Hazard Control Officials roamed the sector complex day and night, watching for any hint of a walking biohazard. It had been years since the last reported case and most people had slipped into happy existences, secure in the belief that the officials were just excuses to create more jobs and that these long years would have been far beyond the longest incubation period the virus had ever displayed.

I, for one, still accepted that it was out there. Or rather much closer to home as events were to transpire. The virus scared me, it scared everyone. A sense of indescribable terror surges through your veins when everything begins to take on that faint red tint. Then the sensation as the first drop of blood trickles from the burst capillaries in the corner of your eye. I slowly placed down the pen on my manuscript as the trickle began to gather on my face. Suddenly it dropped. Dashing a small pool of blood onto my work, rapidly settling into the indentations from the pen. I rose sharply and, cradling my face almost to the point that I couldn't see, ran to the bathroom.

I carefully peeled my hands from my face and gradually gazed through a thick red layer at streams of blood running down my face from the base of my eyes. I grabbed a reel of tissue and desperately wiped the blood from my skin, smearing it across the rest of my face as more swelled up from under my eyelids. As I felt it dry into crusty scabs on my eyelashes a fleeting sense of unpermitted hope crossed my mind, that it was not the horror that had plagued my dreams. The hope quickly shattered when I looked down at the soaked and torn tissues in the sink and quickly realised that, ultimately, I was no stronger then those soft rags of fabric quietly disintegrating on the porcelain. Slowly turning, I returned to the lounge and sat heavily back into my chair, no longer caring about the bloodstains forming on my clothing. If not for the streams of blood continuing down my face I would have liked to think I would have wept. Instead I watched the light dim outside, the oncoming night somehow calming in the way it guided me into sleep. Still it was a haunted sleep; even the release of my mind drifting could not escape that as I knew that there was nothing I could do. The only choice left to me being to turn myself into the containment officers before I become contagious and spare the lives of those around me. As I thought, my sticky eyelids weighed heavily and soon fell closed, condemning me to my restless slumber.

The night rolled on slowly, twisted visions and an intolerable fear haunting my disturbed sleep. Try as I might I could not hold down a length of rest that rescued me from these terrible thoughts. Yet still the floating illusion of sleep seemed to mask the full extent of my terror until, that is, a firm banging raised me from the long dream.

I looked about as daylight poured through my open drapes, burning my weary eyes. Suddenly everything came back to me and I reached up quickly to my face, praying that it had all been some horrifying nightmare. As I felt the crusted blood about my eyelids I gasped in, fighting for breath as my hopes were shattered and the uncontrollable fear again took its firm hold on me. It squeezed around me, restricting my breath as the banging sounded again. It was coming from the door. I pulled my hand away from my face, a shower of crusty blood falling with it, and rushed to the window. I peered around the nets and caught sight of a Hazard Officer before swinging back against the side wall. How did they know?... Officials occasionally dropped in on people for 'Random Inspections' but these days it was more of a social courtesy then anything else. This was different, though, it was no coincidence that much was clear. I considered my options as the officer knocked again, more urgently this time. I knew the right thing to do was to turn myself in before I became contagious and hurt anyone. Instead without thinking I dove across the room as the Officer began hammering constantly on my door. Frantically I clawed the scabs from my face and grabbed a pair of sunglasses to conceal my black eyes. I knew my chances out there were slim. I was going to be dead within a week and I was condemning everyone around me to the same fate. Even as these thoughts were pulsing through my head something continued to defy the nature of my circumstance, telling me not to trust anyone and to run. Looking back at the house I would never see again, I headed for the back door, slipping on the glasses, doing as I had been compelled.

I knew I couldn't stay in the sector; I was only putting its entire population at risk if I did. At this point there was only one choice left. I had to try and make it on the outside. I didn't know what was out there, no one did but it had to be better then vivisection or the multitude of tortures that I felt may be incurred from capture. To this end I waited. The virus infested the bile duct and so victims didn't become contagious until the third day when the vomiting began so I had a maximum of two days. Although with the puss already starting to ooze from under my glasses it didn't seem that long at all. I watched a checkpoint at the edge of the sector where vital deliveries from god only knew where came in to support the populous, waiting for my chance.

I watched the checkpoint for over twelve hours and saw two trucks move in and out of the sector, six hours apart. I had run out of time and, if their schedule held, I had to make a break for one to stow away. As I watched another delivery was perfectly on time. It entered the compound where I hid for several minutes while it was unloaded before turning and heading back out. This is when I struck out and ran as fast I could towards a loose flap in the trailers tarpaulin…I never made it, though. The last I remember is a sharp, stabbing pain in the back of my shoulder and pulling a dart from my skin before falling unconscious.

Now I am here. I don't know how long I was drugged for but from the bruising forming around my eyes I can only assume I was out for at least two days. The sterile cell I now reside in is bleak at the best, the single Plexiglas wall on one side forever threatening the approach of a doctor who sees me nothing more the a specimen, the equivalent of an experiment gone wrong. And yet I realise now that none of that really matters any more, for tomorrow I could be dead.

-Subject 7E-
-Journal Entry 6-

Specimen has been under observation for seventy four hours now and appears to be in the final stages of cellular mutation. Infection within the host is accelerating, as is the breakdown of cognitive processing, resulting in the erratic behaviour displayed at the test site. Prognosis of continued lifespan is no more then twenty hours. Subject displays no increased immunity to the virus but on the merit of the condition remerging after this length of time antidote administration is recommend for continued study of a living specimen.

Additionally the remaining 'Safe Sector' test sites may prove to be of continued value if the virus is, as suggested, undergoing a symbiogenesis within its hosts.

The medical technician placed down her pen and looked to a monitor with the lone subject who was huddled in a corner convulsing gently, his eyes bloody and bruised. She looked away and closed her eyes mournfully before turning and reopening them onto a brightly lit window, looking out over a vast sprawling city. The pointed skyscrapers glinted against the cloudless sky, their affluent majesty a far cry from what the medical prisoner thought to be true.

'I never did agree with the process...Yet they insisted it was necessary' Thought the technician, her mind filled with a sorrow that those involved had tried so hard to forget about. 'They told us the best would be spared and humanities future would be secured, free from overpopulation, famine and every other terrible thing that had plagued our species from the dawn of our existence'. She hung her head in shame for the price that had been paid by those less fortunate 'There were no lucky ones in the end. Even those in the target range who had survived were condemned to live a lie. Nothing more than caged lab rats blindly serving the authoritarian regime, the face in the darkness, for the supposed furthering of the master race'. She looked up again, out at the sprawling megacity. The artificial symbol of what lies and genocide had achieved and finally concluded how monstrous her race had become. "I just hope this finally means we can stop living a tormented lie and at last face up to the terrible deeds we have all become responsible for."

Claudia

It really was unbelievable when I finally experienced it. It still hard to comprehend that it's all as real as it is. How could my life change so much in so little time? I've found out things I could have never even imagined, learnt about myself in a way I didn't think possible. I've gained so much, a view on life like no one else would believe. I've felt loss, though, don't think I haven't. I don't think I will ever be able to let that one go. No matter what else happens, no matter what else I loose, that one is the one that hurt the most...

Tonight the house was silent, void of the echoed screams that usually filled the halls. Claudia's father had obviously drunken himself into enough of a stupor to pass out before he could beat her mother. The quiet was peaceful, relaxing almost. Not so much that Claudia dared to unlock her bedroom door, no, he had risen his hand to her too many times to feel *that* safe. Still, something else kept sleep a longing desire on that night. With the silence she could quiet her mind, let it drift though a void and believe that she was somewhere else. Then there was that itch, a strange sensation deep down in the back of her mind, almost like a voice whispering inside her head. For the life of her she couldn't decipher what it was saying, all she knew was that it was just a voice nestled in her mind, unfettered by the direction of her own thoughts. She opened her eyes and took a sharp breath in, returning to the bitter reality of her life.

The voice lingered for a few seconds, trying to cling on as though it, too, would return to a much worse place if it let go. It wasn't the first time this had happened. Sometimes on the cusp of sleep she would drift into a place where nothing seemed real. It was a place where the voices welled up in her mind and took form, speaking as though part of her own psyche, while the world around her continued to fall further away. The experiences unnerved her but never left her scared, rather curious and intrigued to find out more, yet the next morning it was nothing but a dream.

The phone on Claudia's bedside table suddenly buzzed loudly, making her jump and fumble to answer it before it drew unwanted attention.

"Hello?" she whispered, pulling the phone away for a brief second to see who it actually was. The screen displayed nothing but a seemingly random number, local in area code but nothing else familiar beyond that, "who is this?" she added cautiously.

"Claudia?" came an urgent voice down the phone, "you gotta help me out!"

"Anna?" Claudia queried curiously.

"We were out in the town, then there were these guys and Daz and-"

"Slow down!" whispered Claudia harshly, "what happened?"

"Some of Dazs' dodgy friends turned up and dared him to climb on those old warehouses down the docks," she seemed to choke on her words for a moment, "the roof gave in and he fell. The others did a runner, I didn't know what else to do."

"Stay there," Claudia started without thinking as she got out of bed and quietly began to get dressed, "I'll be there as soon as."

"Thanks, hun," Anna said more softly, "didn't know what else to do," she repeated. "Hurry, though, I don't like this place." The phone went dead and Claudia slipped it into her jeans pocket before heading to the window. From there it was an easy hop down to the shed roof, then into the garden, a simple route she had taken any number of times before when sneaking out.

The night was brisk, making Claudia shiver as she touched down on the overgrown lawn. A jacket would have been a good idea but she daren't risk clambering back into the house just for that. No, the risk of getting caught would have to come later.

Making her way through the dark streets she headed towards the far end of town and the docks, trying to ignore the yobbish gangs hidden out beneath the city's dingy underpasses. Save for a few queer looks she managed to sneak through all but unnoticed, continuing on towards the docklands. Soon enough the silhouettes of high piled cargo containers came into view. Over them loomed the spindly features of cranes against the navy sky with blurred outlines of the ships in the near distance. Claudia quickly slipped through a jagged gap in the docks chain link fence and stepped in tight against the corrugated side of a container. She carefully peered around the side, barely able to see in the shade of the metal towers around her. Slowly she moved away and ventured further towards the waterfront, fearful of who else might be lurking amongst the labyrinth of containers. The yobs in the city were bad but there were people in the docks; strange, depraved, awful people. Some stories even told of wholly unnatural things happening in there, things that logic couldn't explain. Still, some kids thought it was a good place to hang out, have fun, no matter how many of them never came back.

In the distance Claudia managed to see a hazy figure moving slowly back and forth in front a large warehouse. She hesitated for a moment, aware that it could be anyone, and pulled her phone from her pocket, quickly calling back the number that had phoned her. The figure ahead stopped pacing and a faint light appeared around them.

"I take it that's you," whispered Claudia gently, her hushed voice carrying surprisingly far on the chilly air.

The phone went dead and the figure started running towards her.

"Thank god!" said Anna, throwing her arms around Claudia, "this place is freaking me out!" she let go and started looking around wildly.

"New phone?" asked Claudia.

"It's Daz's, mines dead", Anna shifted uneasily. "He got me to hold it before..."

"Where is he?" asked Claudia, eager to get away from the docks as soon as possible.

Anna raised a pointed finger towards the warehouse. "I tried to look in but I couldn't see anything," she looked down and scuffed her pump along the ground. "I shouldn't have let him come. It's just his friends and- I couldn't stop them- I- I just didn't know what to do-," her voice began to choke and a tear trickled down her face. "He'll be ok, won't he?"

"It's alright," Claudia put an arm around Anna's shoulder, "we'll find him and he'll be fine, then we can get out of here so he can do something else stupid," she guided Anna back towards the warehouse and started to walk hurriedly, continuously looking about the area to make sure they hadn't been seen.

The warehouse was apparently much larger than Claudia had expected, as they emerged from behind a large tower of shipping containers. The building stretched far out along the waterfront and had numerous large doors along its face, each defining an individual unit and each locked tightly with a heavy chain and bolt.

"It's this one," whimpered Anna, vaguely pointing to the unit she had been hovering in front of. Claudia quickly let go of her and cautiously shuffled towards a grubby, barred window.

"Why's he always got to get in trouble like this?" Claudia mumbled to herself, peering through a small hole in the window. Inside was pitch black, nothing visible but an indistinct patch of night sky against the roof, obviously where Daz had fallen. For a second she withdrew and fumbled in her jeans pocket before pressing the lit screen of her phone through the hole the best she could while still looking through. The light did little to clear the oppressive darkness, instead merely illuminating the thick cloud of dust that hung, suspended in the warehouse air. Then, after moving the light around, as much as she could, she noticed the shadowy outline of something possibly resembling a person.

"What can you see?" Anna asked weakly, her hand pressed over her mouth, eyes wide open.

Claudia moved her light around a little more before withdrawing again. "It looks like he's out cold," she quickly glanced up at the high roof, "that's a hell of a fall," she added, the concern beginning to show in her voice.

"What're we going to do?" Anna's eyes were still wide open, their white and sky blue a stark contrast to the murky surroundings.

Claudia rose a hand abruptly in an attempt to stop her panicking and delved into another jeans pocket to retrieve a bulky Swiss Army Knife. She proceeded to open out several of the smaller blades and pull a bobby pin from the matt of her, usually straight, raven hair. "These things look tough," she said approaching the large, brass coloured bolt holding the chains together, "just some cheap, mass produced crap, at the end of the day, though," she set to work at picking the lock, something she wasn't all too unfamiliar with, given certain questionable aspects of her youth.

"You don't, seriously, think you'll be able to do it?" Anna stated quickly in hushed tones.

"You tell me," Claudia dropped the heavy lock with a low thud on the soft concrete. She turned back to Anna, holding the chains together to avoid them clattering. "Come help me with this," she fed the chain carefully through the rusted iron handles as Anna laid it gently on the ground. Occasionally the chains chinked together causing a brief moments terror that some unsavoury characters would immediately descend on them. Soon enough the chain was completely off and the large corrugated doors could be heaved open, revealing a wall of dusty blackness.

"Where is he?" Anna slipped into the warehouse as soon as the doors were open wide enough and began searching the darkness, "I've found him!" she shouted from the haze.

"Quiet!" Claudia hissed, stepping quickly inside, "is he alright?" she looked back out of the ajar doors and gazed around again, carefully.

"He's out cold," she reappeared from the shadows briefly, her face full of fear, "what are we going to do?"

Claudia glanced outside one last time before pulling the door together and venturing into the warehouse. "Calm down, everything's going to be fine," she walked over to Anna who hurried back to Daz and stooped over him. In the darkness it was hard to see anything other than a fallen figure and a darkened area around its head.

"I think he's bleeding pretty bad," Anna hovered a hand over his head, not sure how to react.

As her eyes started to adapt to the confined blackness, Claudia began to see Daz's outline more clearly. She bent down to take a closer look, then glanced up at the hole in the high roof. Hanging loosely by a single, frayed rope was a broken pallet which would have broken his fall. Looking back down again she managed to find the rest of the splintered pallet scattered around Daz. Then she realized, having his fall broken like that, he couldn't have been that badly hurt. "It's not his blood," Claudia stated abruptly, "his fall was broken, look," she pointed to the shattered wooden pallet above them.

"He's going to be alright?" Anna asked hopefully as Claudia began to worry about something potentially worse. "Claudia?" she added after a few seconds, when she didn't receive a reply.

"Yeah, yeah, he'll be fine," she looked carefully at the blood stain and noticed it trailed off into the dark warehouse, "probably just have a hell of a headache when he wakes up," she started to follow the trail deeper into the building.

Anna went to edge after her but couldn't bring herself to venture away from Daz. "What are you doing?" she asked without reply, "Cyd?"

Claudia continued to follow the trail far into a corner of the warehouse. It looked almost as though someone had been dragged, bleeding, to a place where no one would notice. Soon, it became too dark for her to see and she started to stumble over her own feet, yet she refused to stop.

"What are you doing?"

"I'm just-" started Claudia but, in a second, realized the voice didn't belong to Anna. Slowly she looked up and peered into the shadows at the edge of the warehouse. There hung a the pale outline of a person, almost translucent against the dusty air. Claudia gradually pivoted her head, trying to keep an eye on the figure but eventually broke her gaze to catch a glance of Anna behind her. She, too, appeared as a mere outline in the darkness but, unlike the other, she was a solid, black shape standing out against the light spilling in from the doorway. Claudia snapped her head back towards the pale apparition which remained motionless against the empty backdrop.

"What are you doing?" it repeated after some time, in a more urgent tone.

The words forced a paralyzing fear to swell up inside Claudia. Thoughts raced through her mind about who it might be, who would hang around inside a pitch black warehouse in the middle of the night? Whoever it was, she thought, they couldn't mean anything good. She tried to back away slowly but stumbled over something and fell to the ground as silently as she could. The fear was now lodged firmly in her throat, forcing her to shake and breath sharply as the figure drifted towards her.

"Are you here to help me?" it asked simply, at last, "I waited but no one came to help."

Suddenly all of the fear was gone, evaporating in lieu of pure curiosity. "Er...Yes," Claudia managed as she pushed herself from the ground, refusing to waver her gaze, "I guess so," she added, not overly sure of how to continue.

"I know what you are. You're like them, but better," the figure continued to advance but never became any clearer. Its shape seemed to be shimmering, its being shifting in and out of the visible spectrum. "You're like me, but alive."

Claudia opened her mouth but no words were produced. The figure finally stopped in front of her, no more visible than it had ever been, and leaned towards her. From the darkness, out of the shimmering silhouette before her, a face seemed to press through the air, like an invisible barrier had been blocking her view. The face was that of a young man, barely older than Claudia, but it was deformed with horrific scars and bruising, like he had been tortured.

"Take it, take it back," he said firmly, "the stone. Undo their corruption and free us," he looked deep into Claudia eyes with intense meaning, "please." His image faded again and soon his entire body drifted into the ether, leaving nothing but confusion in Claudia's mind.

She knew she had to leave, right now, get away from there, never look back and forget the night had ever happened. Yet, against all reason she was compelled to stay. Her feet were more than ready to turn heel and run but she was drawn forward to a workbench pushed up against the metal side of the building. Acting as though she had been there before, she reached forward and switched on an overhead lamp. The bright light stung her eyes for a few seconds, blinding her to what was there. Without knowledge of her own actions she cocked her head to one side and bent down. As her sight started to clear it became apparent there was a storage space underneath the desk. Only instead of being filled with tools and equipment it had a body stuffed into it, broken and bent into contorted positions just to fit it in. Claudia gasped and fell back again into the trail of blood she had followed. Then it all came back, the fear, the shaking. She scrambled to get away from the sticky trail in the dust and huddled herself against another workbench, staring at her bloodied hands.

"Are you alright over there?" came Anna's hushed voice, at last, easing the tension slightly. "We should get going."

"Yeah," Claudia said with a stunted breath, "Yeah, in a minute," she added, more calmly, turning her attention to the body under the desk. She refused to believe it but the body was the young mans, the one who she had seen like a ghost. Like a bolt of lightning the truth struck her, a truth her mind immediately rejected and refused to accept on any account. Even so, the more she thought about it the more she knew it to be so. He *was* a ghost, or at least as close as you can get to one. Still, her mind refuted the idea even though her heart seemed to accept it so readily, like it was as natural a concept as the sun rising. Continuing to stare at the gruesome scene for a minute or two more, Claudia noticed something clasped in the corpses' hand, something grey, a stone maybe. Could this have been what he was talking about? Eventually coming to terms with the scene, she crept towards the storage shelf and the body. The shelf was dripping with half congealed blood and had the wretched air of putrefaction. Every breath made her gag a little more but she eventually brought herself to reach over to the mans tightly clenched fist and wrench it from the mass of twisted flesh. The fist fell from the shelf loosely and hit the ground with a thud but didn't open any. Claudia sighed, knowing what she had to do but unknowing of why she was doing it. She grasped his wrist firmly and jammed her fingers behind his, pulling at them until they came loose with a combination of popping and cracking sounds. The sounds made her shudder and retch but out of his broken hand fell a polished, oval granite stone. On one side was carved an odd symbol with vertical parallel lines and a horizontal tilde between them, intersecting a darkly tinted fragment of Smokey Quartz in its centre.

She gazed at the object for a second. It seemed to make the air around it shimmer as though it were incredibly hot, yet there was no warmth to deter the chilly night. Quickly, she snatched up the stone and hurried back towards Anna and the murky light of the ajar entrance. By this time Anna had managed to rouse Daz, who was furiously complaining, confused at what had happened to him.

"Just keep your damn voice down!" snapped Anna, helping Daz from the ground.

"Oh, aye, here she is!" he moaned loudly, pointing at Claudia's figure emerging from the back of the warehouse, "thought you'd have something to do with this. Trouble you are!"

Anna grimaced and slapped Daz on the arm. "She came to help you!"

"Some help," Daz started aggressively, "she can't even help herself," he continued pointing at her accusingly, "I know about your Mum!"

Claudia gritted her teeth and punched away his outstretched arm grabbing his coat tightly, "Listen! You're lucky to be alive! You got yourself into this, you ungrateful git! I'm just here because of her," without breaking eye contact she threw her arm towards Anna, "if you didn't go pissing around with those little shits than none of us would be here!" she pushed him away and breathed out heavily. "I remember when you used to be alright," she ended simply, "where did he go?"

Daz looked at the ground, daring not to say anything further.

"That's what I thought," added Claudia, shoving past him, "we'd better get going."

"What did you find over there?" Anna asked as she caught up with Claudia, leaving Daz to tail behind.

"Nothing," she stated quickly, slipping the stone into her back pocket, "just some work benches," she hated to lie to Anna but thought that what she had really found was better off something kept to herself.

"I'm sorry about Daz," Anna murmured solemnly, sidling in front of Claudia, "he thinks he's clever saying stuff like that. Don't know why I hang around with the idiot...I just couldn't leave him, though, he could have been really hurt."

"It's alright," Claudia stopped and run the back of her hand over Anna's cheek, "you did the right thing. Someone has to do the right thing, even if others can't," she rolled her eyes back towards Daz who grumbled quietly.

"Thanks, Cyd," she turned and pulled the warehouse door open again but as soon as she did a hand reached through and grabbed her hair, dragging her out into the open.

"Anna!" Claudia quickly went to dive for the assailant but was caught by the arm by another hand who pulled her out and threw her to the ground.

"What do you think you're doing here?" growled a voice from above, "this isn't a tourist attraction, you know!"

Claudia blew a wisp of hair from her face and looked over to Anna. She was still being grasped by the hair, held on her knees by a lean, unstable looking man. "We're no one," she answered at last, not sure anything she could say would have been ideal.

"No one?" the man above her snapped again, "break into our warehouse and you're 'no one?'"

Claudia finally turned to look at her attacker but all she could see was a short, bulky silhouette against the yellow tinted city sky. She glanced over to the doorway, finally, to see Daz creeping up on it. She raised her eyebrows at him expectantly but received nothing back but an off hand shrug.

"How much did you see?" the other man said, pulling on Anna's hair, making her whimper slightly.

"Nothing!" stated Claudia loudly, pushing out her open palm in the hopes of stopping him.

The shorter silhouette stooped down over Claudia, somewhat uncomfortably, and sighed. "Come on, you expect we believe that after you quite obviously broke in and started snooping around?" his voice was calm, almost soothing in a way, which made it all the more concerning. "Now, who sent you and what did you see in there?"

There was silence for a few seconds before the unstable man pulled at Anna's hair again. "Who?!"

"We just come to get our friend!" cried out Anna, close to tears, "he fell through the roof and we couldn't get to him without breaking in..." she tailed off and slumped to the ground, sobbing, as her capture loosened his grip.

"He?" questioned the silhouette, looking to his colleague uneasily.

"Me!" shouted Daz loudly, darting from the building and running off into the maze of cargo containers, with the men quickly jumping into pursuit.

"Come on!" said Claudia, quickly grabbing Anna's arm to pull her up, forcing her to start running in the opposite direction to Daz.

"What about-?" Anna tried.

"He'll be fine," she looked back briefly to reassure Anna, "trust me."

After some time they found themselves back on the main road, rounding the edge of the docks. Although they were still far from safe, they were, at the very least, out of immediate danger.

"Who the hell were those guys?" panted Anna, jogging to a stop.

"I'm not sure I want to know," Claudia replied as she leant up against a lamp post, breathing heavily. "I guess they owned the warehouse, though."

"When you say 'own' I assume you mean use as a front for organized crime," Anna chuckled to herself, trying to raise her spirits.

"Yeah," Claudia croaked uneasily, not so amused, knowing that this was something much more sinister than mere organized crime. "Look," she started again, seriously, "get home as quick as you can, make sure no one follows you. Just... forget this night ever happened."

Anna nodded gently and was about to run off but instead turned back again. "Thanks for coming, don't know what I'd do without you," she started walking backwards, out of the streetlamps warm pool of light. "I just hope Daz got away alright, too."

As Anna started off into the night Claudia considered what she had said. Things had changed tonight, her very perception of reality had been shaken by what could only be described as a ghost. Not to mention loosing what little innocence she had left by witnessing what had happened to that ghosts mangled body. Yet it could have all been avoided by staying home. Still, it was over now, she just wanted to forget about it all and carry on. Only she couldn't do that. As she reached into her back pocket and touched the stone she had found, that same feeling which had compelled her to take it in the first place, told her she couldn't just go back to the way things were. Something had started, something that would come to define her and no matter what she wanted, it could not be stopped.

Claudia pulled her hand away from the stone and shuddered, before, herself, disappearing into the darkness towards home and an uncertain welcome.

With the creeping dawn beginning to crest in the distance, an aging, rusted car rolled into a narrow, cobbled backstreet and creaked to a halt. Almost involuntarily the engine sputtered to silence and both front doors swung open simultaneously. The two men who had set after chasing Daz, again simultaneously, stepped from the car and strolled around to the boot, slamming their doors as they went. There were thuds and muffled moaning coming from inside, which made the men turn to each other and grin. After several seconds of their perverse enjoyment, the taller of the two popped open the lid to reveal Daz, crammed into the small boot, his limbs bound and a sack pulled over his head. He had obviously been kicking at the side in a vain attempt to draw some attention but stopped as soon as the lid cracked open. Instead, he waited for one of the men to reach into retrieve him and kicked out blindly in the hopes of catching one, or both, of his captures unaware. Despite his best attempts the lean man managed to dodge his attacks and grab his legs under an arm, continuing on to punch Daz firmly in the stomach.

"Nice try, son!" the short man stated, laughing as his colleague gritted his teeth, tempted to get another punch in while he could, "but you're not gonna get one over on us that easy," he reached down and grabbed Daz by the collar, wrenching him from the car and allowing him to flop limply to the hard cobbles.

"Why don't we just do him now?" asked the unstable one, eagerly, "say something just 'happened,'" he reached for a hunting knife, stashed in his coat pocket but was stopped by a stubby fingered hand.

"Boss'll want him alive. Seeing as how those other two got away, he's the only one who can tell us anything," he gave Daz a gentle kick, making him squirm slightly, still reeling from the sucker punch. "Besides, I'm sure the boss'll have something much more...creative in mind than that little thing," he glanced at the half drawn knife and grinned again.

With the knife replaced the lean man grabbed Daz again and dragged him towards a rotten wooden door, what remaining paint left on it curling up and flaking away. He hammered on it for a second with his fist, making shards of soft wood fall away, and held his captive up to a seldom seen peephole, high in the door.

In prompt manner, locks were removed on the other side and the door was swung open by another individual of questionable mental status. He watched as the two men dragged Daz through the entrance, eyes wide, trembling gently. As soon as they were through he slammed the door and replaced the locks quickly before turning back. "He'll like this one," he stated simply, half a smile curling up at the side of his lips, "looks like he'd cut well."

"I'm sure *he* will," replied the shorter man, staring the doorman down, "but you won't!" he ended sternly, returning to drag Daz away.

The building was, as far as what remained could define, an old nightclub. It had been abandoned over a decade prior and become one of those forgotten relics of a past era. A place so accepted in the state it was in that it wasn't even acknowledged by kids looking for a hangout. Only junkies and drug addicts gave the place the time of day, the feeble minded caring only about their next fix. Undesirables to most, some would find the simple influence one could have over these people as an inviting opportunity.

After being dragged over what was left of the dance floor, with every single half lucid junkie staring at him, Daz was taken into one of the back rooms and dropped in front of a simple, stained sofa. Filthy, as it was, compared to everything else in that place, it was likely the plushest thing around.

As Daz struggled to get to his knees, the sack was pulled roughly from his head and his dingy surroundings were blinding compared to beneath the thick sack. His face was covered with bruises, the black eyes and fat lip evidence enough of how he had been subdued. He looked around wildly, the sudden sting in his nostrils of that rotten stench; of urine and decaying humanity only inciting his fear yet more. Behind him the residents of the building peered curiously through the tattered curtain over the doorway. Either side of him were tables filled with unique and unusual objects, much too fantastic to belong in this place. Among them, positioned in the forefront, was a stone tablet with four ornate stones, each emblazoned with strange glyphs and a gem in their centres. In the middle of the tablet, though, there was simply an empty hole, as if one of the stones was missing. Before he could get a better look at any of the objects, though, another tatty curtain to the side of the sofa twitched. Just then all of the eyes watching him from behind disappeared, afraid of whatever was entering the small room.

"What requires my attention, now?" stated a surprisingly calm voice through the curtain, "I do not enjoy these interruptions," the voice had an unusual air about it. A Central American tone but dulled by decades away from its home, mixed with influences from innumerous other dialects.

"We found this kid in the warehouse," said the shorter of the two men, deciding not to complicate the situation by mentioning Claudia and Anna.

The curtain was finally pulled aside and a tall, muscular man stepped out towards the sofa. His tanned skin was wrinkled and creased as though he was of some considerable age yet only his dark, sunken eyes told of how considerable it could really be. He gently sat on the sofa as though it were some throne of sorts and leant forward to inspect Daz. After a second he glanced up and between his henchmen before, at last, leaning back without speaking.

"You dealt with our other concern?" he asked eventually, seeming not to care about the boy in front of him, "and retrieved the item?"

"We tied up the loose end..." the short man said tentatively.

"Excellent. Yet I feel there is something else?"

The henchman hesitated, his mouth hung open. "It wasn't there," he looked down to Daz and grimaced, "I think he took it."

The old man only now took proper notice of Daz and looked over him at a distance. "Who are you?" he asked. "You're no one. Wrong place, wrong time," he added before Daz could speak. He reached out and pulled Dazs' chin up so that he could look in his eyes. "This child did not take the artefact," the statement made the henchmen quickly share a glance, each of them afraid of their failure to capture the two girls, "he is not one of them."

"There were others-" spurted the lean man only to be cut off by his employer.

"I know," he continued to look into Dazs' eyes, "two of them...Women. One is of no importance. The other though..." he looked up and grinned a disturbing grin, "our new friend, here, will tell us all about her..."

Claudia carefully unlocked her back gate and stepped into her garden, replacing the catch as quietly as she could. She looked up at her ajar bedroom window and considered the best way to get back in. Despite the fact that getting down was routine and easy, getting back up again had always been troublesome and was never quite achieved in the same way twice. The problem was rendered moot though, as the kitchen light flickered on and Claudia immediately knew the night was about to go from bad to worse. The back door was pulled open quickly, as if by an unseen force, and she hurried towards the small gap. The second she was in the door was quietly swung closed and Claudia's mother was stood there. Disapproval was hinted at thinly across her haggard face but it was smothered by an overwhelming concern.

"What were you doing out there?" she whispered harshly constantly glancing towards the bottom of the stairs, "I've been worried sick!"

Claudia looked down, unsure of how to respond after the night she had experienced. "Just been out with some friends," she answered generically.

Her mother seemed less than impressed at the statement and raised her eyebrows expectantly. "Out with friends? You know what could happen to you out there? The kind of trouble you could get into?"

"I'm nearly eighteen years old, mum, I can look after myself," Claudia interrupted abruptly to no avail.

"Moreover," her mother continued unfettered, "you know the kind of trouble you could cause us here? It's lucky you didn't wake your father!"

"What if she did?" came a deep voice from the darkened stairs, "is that some kind of a problem?" Claudia's father stepped silently from the bottom stair and moved into the light of the kitchen. On the face of it he looked like any average man, capable of going about a normal life like everyone else. Yet, something deep in his eyes told a different story. A man whose view of reality was as he decided to perceive it, a man with a talent to twist the truths of circumstance to fit his own deluded view.

"I-I- just-" Claudia's mother stuttered, "didn't want to wake you," she looked around nervously and tried an uneasy smile. "No point waking you for this."

He smiled back widely, which only acted to raise the tension yet more rather than relieve it. "It's no problem. I'll handle it."

"I swear it's no-"

"I said I'll handle it!" Claudia's father growled, grabbing her wrist tightly, squeezing tighter until she whimpered in pain.

"Leave her alone!" Claudia tried firmly without response, "please."

Eventually he released her arm and looked down at the mark he had left which was already beginning to bruise, "you know you shouldn't wear that watch of yours so tight," his attention turned sharply to Claudia and he struck out, catching her by the arm, "as for you! I give you food and a roof over your head!" he abruptly slapped her about the face, quickly holding her other arm as she tried to retaliate.

"No, please! Not her," Claudia's mother tried to pull him away but was caught in the jaw by his fist as he, again, turned his attention.

"Mum," whispered Claudia only to receive a shaking head from her mother as she was forced to the ground. This wasn't the first time this had happened and she knew just to run to her room and lock the door so that's exactly what she did. Backing up against the far wall of her bedroom she held her arms close against herself and tried not to listen to the muffled screams and shouted slurs. Closing her eyes she reached for the knife that was still in her pocket and considered ending it, like she had many times before. Then that thought crept into her mind. Everyone loved him, as far as the outside world was concerned he was wonderful, it would be her mother who got the blame. As always she withdrew her hand and sank to the ground, wrapping her arms around her knees. Suddenly there was a loud bang and silence, then heavy feet climbing the creaking stairs. She listened carefully for a minute or so longer and finally heard a gentle sobbing from downstairs. Despite her anguish she was relieved, for everything else that had happened her mother had at the very least survived. Something, she feared, that would not last forever. Once again she thought about that knife and its potential, knowing something might have to happen, and soon. For now, though, she slumped down further, reluctantly closing her eyes, and hoped that sleep might take her to a better place.

Occasionally, during the night, Claudia managed to drift away into a restless land of lucid dreams. The place was filled with death and the moans of those who yearned for life once more. Upon being roused from the state she felt as if she had not been asleep at all, like an entirely different world had snatched her attention away, unwilling to return it. Each time it slowly drew her back. Wide eyed, blinking, the tangible world drifted away and the un-summoned thoughts crept into her mind, the spoken word of another's consciousness.

Suddenly she was started from the trance by a clatter outside. Sun poured through her, still open, window, burning her eyes as they adjusted to the new day. She didn't care how early it was, the mere fact that it was morning gave her an excuse to get away from the house. Quickly, she gathered up some notepads strewn around the room and threw them loosely into a backpack before approaching the door carefully. She couldn't hear anything out there, likelihood was that her father was still asleep. With this in mind she opened the door, hurried down the stairs and slipped through the front door, out into the frosty street, without even looking back.

As she started off along the road towards College, Claudia thought about the previous night. Everything had happened so quickly, none of it making any sense. She touched her pack pocket and the stone that still sat there, thinking about the body she had retrieved it from. Did she remember it wrong? Was he actually still alive when he spoke to her? It was something her mind couldn't quite come to understand, something it tried to twist at all costs to make sense. Only, she knew what she had seen and no amount of twisting could change that.

For the most part the rest of the day went by like any other; a few lessons before lunch then to hang out in the library before meeting Anna in the afternoon. Although, today, instead of just sitting around, messing on her phone, Claudia ventured into the rows upon rows of bookshelves, stone in hand, curious about what the markings on it could mean. Book after book, the table she was sat at began to pile up with various tomes on ancient history, notably that of Meso and South American cultures. As the hours started to slip by, so did Claudia's hope of finding something meaningful in the texts, anything to give the item any meaning.

"Hey Cyd," Anna's voice said cheerfully, startling Claudia slightly, "not like you to be studying this hard," she fell down on a chair behind the piles of books and started flicking through one.

"It's not work," Claudia replied simply, "just some research."

"Research?" Anna asked, suspiciously, knowing it wasn't a word either of them used lightly, if at all.

Claudia sighed and reached into her pocket, withdrawing the stone. Somehow it looked different in the daylight, not quite as meaningful as it had the previous night. She held it for a second, doubting its significance, only to finally toss it onto the page of Anna's open book. "I found it last night..." she leant across the table and whispered, "in the warehouse."

Anna picked up the stone and inspected it, running her thumb over the dark grooves in its surface. "In the warehouse?" she repeated.

"T- That's not all of it..." Claudia paused for a second, debating just how much to tell her, "I found it on...it was on a dead guy," she practically mouthed the words, quickly swivelling her eyes around the room as she spoke.

"Dead?!" Anna choked, fumbling with the book but drawing no attention, "you mean..."

"Dead...Throat slit..." she shuddered as she spoke the words. Actually saying them seemed to make the whole situation all that more real.

"You didn't tell me this?" Anna growled quietly, "just wander off, find a dead guy and don't tell anyone?"

"It was complicated. What with those men and all," she sighed again and leaned back in her chair. "Thought they might've been antiques smugglers or something so I wanted to know what it was. Can't find anything on the damn thing, though!"

"Really?" asked Anna subtly, "you obviously haven't been looking hard enough, then" she handed a book back over to Claudia with the stone perched on one of the pages.

"Typical," she stated softly looking down at the book. Anna had placed the stone on top of a rough drawing of its self with two more stones either side, each having a different marking on it, "trust you to find it straight off."

"It was right there, Cyd, you must have overlooked it."

"Hmm," Claudia replied absently, skimming over the text, "needed a fresh pair of eyes. I didn't get much sleep last night."

"Again?" Anna inquired only to receive a brief glance across the book which told her not to push the topic any further.

"'Purportedly originating from early pre-Columbian Meso-America,'" she read slowly, "'the Fragments of Essence, or more commonly Soul Stones as they came to be called, were held in the highest regard by certain castes of society. They were said to possess the power to drain life from the living or return it to the dead,'" Claudia looked up sideways at Anna who shrugged, unknowing of what she had seen. "'The worshipers of these stones were held as heretics, shunned by others for their use of, what was considered, black magic.' It goes on to say that each stone supposedly had a unique power," she skimmed the text a bit more as Anna leaned over, curious, "but they hadn't been seen in over a century before this book was written."

"Looks like a pretty old book, too," Anna mused to herself. "I guess they were treasure hunters or antiques thieves or whatever. That-" she waved her arm around, scrunching up her face in disgust, "dead person probably just got in their way."

"Yeah..." Claudia stretched out the word, knowing for definite there was something more to the whole thing now. What with the ghost and these stones having something to do with life and death she found herself coming to believe in something she never would have even considered before.

"They're not going to give up, Anna. Those men. If they want this thing that bad they're going to track us down. I need to go back to the warehouse, replace the stone. Maybe if they found it again they wouldn't look for us." Despite the truth in this, it wasn't nearly the whole reason she wanted to go back. Claudia wanted to find out more, some compulsion drove her to want find out what the stones really were and even have another experience with the world of the dead. Yet, still, she didn't want Anna involved with any of it. As far as Claudia was concerned she already knew too much. Anna would never let her go alone, yet she had to try. "I'll go down now, just put it back like it fell on the ground and they didn't see it. You stay here, I'll be back soon," she quickly got up, hoping that if it all happened fast enough then Anna would stay where she was but just as she expected a hand grabbed her arm gently.

"Like hell you're going off without me. We were both there last night so we both do this."

"Seriously, Anna, I'll be fine. Won't be more than an hour," she tried again in earnest.

"No," Anna replied firmly, looking deep into Claudia's eyes, "we're both going. Besides, it should be perfectly safe during the day.

"S'pose," Claudia conceded, beginning to think that simply taking the stone back and not hanging around was probably the best idea, "just hope they haven't put a better lock on that place."

By the time they reached the docks the dark autumn evening had began to close in, leaving a cold bite in the air and a dull blue haze in the sky. As it was, a new bolt had not been put on the warehouse doors. In fact the doors hadn't even been locked again, merely pushed loosely together for anyone to open.

"So much for security," said Anna softly, inspecting the door casually.

"I don't like it, they wouldn't just leave them open, not with what's in there," Claudia caught Anna's arm as she was about to pull open the door.

"Could've moved it," Anna stated simply, "it'd make sense, especially after someone found it."

Claudia thought for a second before pressing in front of Anna. "I guess you're right, but just let me go first, will you?" she quietly pulled open the large door and ventured inside. In the dull afternoon light the warehouse appeared much smaller than it had the night before. The back walls were now clearly in view, each lined with various benches and tool racks. On the ground there, still, laid broken fragments of wood and a scuffed up patch of dirt where Daz had fallen. Just behind it was the blood trail leading to the workbench where Claudia had seen the ghost and found the stone. As Anna had suggested, the body had been moved. All that was left were smears of blood across the painted metal.

"Just dropping it here should do," Claudia mused, moving over to the workbench, "they'll think it was just dropped or something," she bent down and was about to toss the stone onto the ground but was stopped by a scuffle from behind her. "Anna?" she started, catching a sharp blow to the back of the head before she could turn, knocking her on to the ground, unconscious.

The darkness span and twisted, forcing up a sickly feeling from Claudia's stomach which spread out around the back of her head and deepened into her skull. Soon enough she started to hear muffled voices around her and tried to open her eyes as the throbbing in her head grew.

"It's those bitches from last night," came one voice, moving around rapidly.

"...Bring me the artefact," sounded another accented voice softly. For a while the words hazed in and out as Claudia fought for consciousness. Eventually, though, she was snapped back into it by a hand grabbing her collar and yanking her across the ground. A second later she was dropped again and, as she looked around with a drifting, unsteady sight, she could see a heavily built man standing in front of her. After seeming to look at her for a moment he stepped to one side and began inspect something else. Trying to recover her faculties, Claudia forced her head up and looked to the side. She could see the man looking carefully at Anna, who seemed as dazed as she did. To one side stood one of their assailants from the previous night, apparently awaiting a command.

"This one is no good," came the voice in that warped Central American drole. His words prompted the man next to him to quickly react, raising his arm with something clasped in his hand.

"No!" screamed Claudia, catching a glint from the gun through her painful haze. Her cry, though, was immediately silenced by the gunshot and a low thud on the ground next to her. There was a sensation like water trickling down the side of her face making her shiver. Even in her current state, she knew it was anything but water.

"You are special, I think," the mans voice sounded again, this time directed towards Claudia, unmoved by what had just happened, "but you have not yet explored your potential," he paused, awaiting an answer.

Claudia breathed heavily, her eyes closed tight so that she did not have to see. "You-" she tried, choking on the meaning of the words, "killed..." she hung her head to one side, desperate to cry but could not.

The man shook his head and signalled to his other subordinate who brought over the stone tablet, now housing all five stones. "I feel you should know why. Know what all of this means," he stated flatly, "you, at least, deserve that," he picked up the central stone and moved it between his fingers. "There is more to reality than you would know. Life, death...not as fixed as you would think. There are worlds between, where the dead pass before reaching their final destination. Some of us, like me... and you, are able to traverse these worlds. The problem is that, like life, our time in those worlds is finite," he reached down and held the stone in front of Claudia's face but her eyes were still sealed tightly. "I made these stones very long ago to try and change that. All those people who had the power but not the knowledge to use it... Well, I simply refocused that power."

"You stole their lives?" murmured Claudia.

"Stole is such a harsh term, I prefer to say I utilized their potential. How else do you think I made it over seven hundred years?" the man said cheerfully. "See, that's the thing with our kind. We have that inherent knowledge of the greater scheme of things and a drive to find out what it is we can become. You see, though, the process cannot be completed unless all stones are together. Take one, take all. Such a waste, he was like us, you know, but that little bastard had it coming for stealing what was mine."

"The ghost..." Claudia mumbled, opening her eyes, looking up.

"Met him, did you?" he said grinning, moving the stone towards her head. As it got closer it started to glow, the others still in their tablet following suit.

"He said to bring it back," she ended, staring at the man who would steal her very life.

"What?" the mans grin fell away as the stone touched Claudia's skin and he realized it was too late, "what did he do?"

There was a burst of the whitest light and Claudia felt her body fall away. Her surroundings shifted and blurred, eventually settling back into their own form. In front of her still stood the man, arm outstretched but with nothing in hand. Around her the scenery was dull and washed out, various parts of the walls shimmered as if unsure if they should be there or not. The more she looked around, the more one word embedded its self in her mind; "Desert," she mouthed. "He tricked you, didn't he?"

"I cannot be tricked!" the man stated defiantly, "after seven centuries it is not possible!"

"You know it is," another voice suddenly started from behind, making Claudia shift around quickly, "and I did it," the voice belonged to the ghost she had seen the night before. "I knew you would hunt her and eventually use the stone on her. I'm just glad my, ahem, modifications worked. Instead of draining her essence, the artefact is now, instead, draining yours into her," he approached Claudia and smiled widely. "You'll be ok."

"This cannot be happening," the man said simply, not knowing what to do as he felt his own life slipping away, "I cannot die... I cannot..." he repeated as his figure faded and his being started to drift into the beyond.

"Wha-" Claudia tried to ask, overwhelmed by everything that was happening.

"I'm sorry to have used you like this. It was my intention that no one else got caught up in the plan, that merely the next time he tried to use it..." the young man sighed, "well, you know, best laid plans and all that. But I *am* sorry for everything, especially her," he looked down at the place where Anna had fallen. "It can't be for long, I barely have any time left here myself but I can just about give you this," he closed his eyes and faded away, only to be replaced by the spirit of Anna, looking as bewildered as Claudia felt.

"Cyd?" Anna asked softly, just to be shushed by Claudia who threw her arms around her and held her tight.

"Remember this," Claudia whispered, "remember us," she added, holding tight for a moment before her arms folded onto herself and Anna disappeared before her.

"I'm sorry. I couldn't hold her here any longer," the young man's voice said quietly. "I'm afraid you need to be going now as well."

Claudia eventually lowered her arms and opened her eyes, a tear finally running down her face as she did. "What am I?"

The young man thought about saying the words but decided that, when considering everything that had happened to their kind, it was better not to. "You're not alone," he settled on after a few seconds, "you'll never be alone," he placed a hand softly on Claudia's face and the light, again, took her away.

When I woke up the young mans ghost was nowhere to be seen and the two goons had gone. Apparently they weren't as hard as they thought, not without a leader. There I was in that dark warehouse again where it had all started, everyone dead but me. I couldn't bring myself to look at Anna, not in that way, I just closed my eyes and remembered her in my arms. What else could I do after that? I phoned the police. They had plenty of questions but eventually released me, putting the case down to 'Organized Crime.' Something I'd come to find out they did pretty often. The whole experience left me with something, the knowledge of something more, something for all of us. With that in mind I wrote Mum that letter and left it with a train ticket to anywhere he couldn't find her. I never found out whether she used it or not, I couldn't stay any longer. That feeling was taking me over, that urge to learn what I was, what I could be. So I left, left everything I knew to find them... To find myself.

Printed in Great Britain
by Amazon

11049297R00062